BELL LANE
LONDON E1

By Kim Hunter

Kim Hunter

Copyright © 2013 By Kim Hunter

The right of Kim Hunter to be identified as author of this work has been asserted in accordance with sections 77 and 78 of the Copyright, Designs and Patents Act 1988.

All rights Reserved
No reproduction, copy or transmission of this publication
may be made without written permission.
No paragraph of this publication may be reproduced,
Copied or transmitted save with the written permission of the author, or in
accordance with the provisions of the Copyright Act 1956 (as amended)

This is a work of fiction.
Names, places, characters and incidents originate from the writers imagination.
Any resemblance to actual persons, living or dead is purely coincidental.

OTHER WORKS BY KIM HUNTER

EAST END HONOUR
WHATEVER IT TAKES
TRAFFICKED
EAST END LEGACY
EAST END A FAMILY OF STEEL
PHILLIMORE PLACE LONDON

Web site www.kimhunterauthor.com

PREFACE

"I've lived to almost eighty five Billy Boy and do you know what I've learned? That human beings are shits, that they hurt each other just because they can. The one piece of advice I can give you, is that every action has a reaction. Think long and hard before you hurt anyone Billy Boy because the repercussions could ruin the rest of your life."

**Dulcie Gray
(1927 - 2011)**

PROLOGUE
Midnight February 14th 2012

Olivia Jacobs opened the front door and marched into the hall. She threw her handbag onto the floor and slammed the door shut. Not caring who she woke up, Olivia stomped up the stairs. Sally Jacobs shook the arm of her husband who was snoring softly.
"Billy! Billy wake up."
"Not tonight Sal, I'm tired."
"Billy! Livy's just come in and I think she's been drinking."
Billy Jacobs rubbed at his eyes with the back of his hands.
"Sal she's eighteen now, you've got to cut her a bit of slack."
Sally shoved her husband hard in the back, a signal that she wasn't going to let the matter drop.
"She might be eighteen but I remember when we were that age, don't you? Or now that you're some hot shot manager have you conveniently forgotten?"
"Alright, alright I'll go and see if she's ok, now go back to sleep. Honest to god I don't think you two will ever let me have any fucking peace!"
Pulling on his dressing gown Billy walked along the landing to his daughter's room. Tapping lightly he didn't wait to be invited in. Olivia Jacobs lay on the bed facing the wall, she had her back to her father

and when he came in, didn't attempt to turn round.
"What?"
"You mum thinks you've been drinking."
Olivia quickly turned over on the bed and Billy instantly knew that she was in a strop.
"I aint had a drop! Here smell me breath?"
"Then what's the matter sweetheart? Why did you come stomping in the house like a two ton bleeding elephant?"
"It's that fucking Lucy Clarke."
"Language Livy!"
"Sorry but she really pisses me off Dad! Me and Tommy Smith, well we've been getting to know each other lately and I really like him. That bitch Lucy only went off with him tonight, well I know just how to teach her a lesson! I think I'll tell everyone she sleeps about, that'll wipe the smile of her face."
"I thought Lucy was your best pal?"
"Huh! I don't think so. I am going to go on face book and put the record straight dad, no one bleeding shafts me and gets away with it."
Smiling to himself Billy gently sat down on the side of his daughter's bed.
"Can I tell you a story?"
"I aint five dad!"
"I know you aint darling but just this once would you humour your old man?"
Olivia Jacobs didn't reply and picking up her mobile began to text some imaginary friend. Undeterred Billy carried on talking and within five minutes the

mobile lay on the bed and Olivia Jacobs hung on her father's every word.

CHAPTER ONE
1992

Born in nineteen seventy two, Billy Jacobs was the only son of Jackie Lemon. A noisy boy who always had something to say, he quickly became what the authorities preferred to call, a difficult child. In reality Billy just wanted to be liked but his incessant questions and bad behaviour saw him expelled from school by the age of fourteen. His mother had given birth to Billy while she was still at school and even though it had been frowned upon, Jackie had been adamant that she was keeping him. Times were hard and after her family had all but abandoned her, Jackie Lemon had been forced to hold down three jobs for most of Billy's childhood. From a young age, much too young as far as the law was concerned, Billy was left alone. His mother didn't see him as a latchkey kid and when he complained of coming home to an empty house, she would only say that it was how things were and he would just have to get on with it. Apart from taking his father's name Billy didn't know who the man was and even though he continually plagued his mother to reveal more details, she would just stare at him blankly. As a small boy her refusal to name his father only fuelled Billy's curiosity. After riffling through the few personal possessions his mother owned, he'd come up with a big fat zero so Billy had relied on fantasy. The young boy would spend hours laying on his bed making up stories about millionaires and mercenaries until he finally found a tale he was happy with. When anyone ever asked him about his parents, Billy Jacobs would tell them his father was called Kevin and he was an airline pilot who worked in America and had a really big house with servants. No one believed him, they only had to look at where he lived and the way he was dressed to know that his story was nothing but a pack of lies. Still, the make believe kept him happy until he reached his teens. Puberty changed Billy Jacobs and almost overnight he became rude and obnoxious to anyone who gave him the time of day and that included his mother.

Jackie called out to Billy who was still curled up in bed.

"I'm off now!"

There was no reply and Jackie spoke out as she left "Might as well talk to me bleeding self."

Starting out at six each morning she would make her way from their flat in Ellingfort Road over to the council building on Flanders way. If Jackie walked quickly the journey could be done in thirty minutes but most days she preferred to walk slowly. Her shift didn't start until seven so time wasn't a problem. The problem was her life, a life which Jackie hated. She hated her flat, her past and at times she even hated her son. After three hours of cleaning she would return home exhausted and wait for the time to pass until she had to start her next job. It had been this way ever since the day Billy had started school. Now fourteen years later and nothing had changed but Jackie and her son somehow seemed to muddle along together.

At almost twenty years old and with no job, Billy spent his time sprawled on the sofa or dossing about the Streets, up to no good. Months of nagging and telling him to pull his socks up had achieved absolutely nothing and it was getting Jackie down. The thought had crossed her mind to kick him out but then it wouldn't solve anything and she would only be putting her problems onto someone else. Oh he wasn't a bad lad, not really, but sometimes it felt as though she was banging her head against a brick wall whenever she tried to talk to him.

Home again and with just over an hour before her next shift down at the local supermarket began, Jackie needed that time to relax and enjoy a cuppa. With Billy lying on the sofa smoking endless cigarettes and with mind numbing music blaring out, relaxing was almost impossible. Most days she would just shake her head, pull on her coat and go straight back out again. Jackie Lemon would rather spend her time down at Harry's cafe than be in her own sons company.

From the supermarket she would return home, prepare Billy's dinner and then be out again by six thirty. Today she was late for her shift at the local cinema, her last job of the day. Old Timpson had been on her back since she'd first got the job. If she was late again tonight it would give him the chance to sack her and that thought scared Jackie. She wasn't scared about losing the money, only the time that she would have to fill and which would most likely have to be spent in the company of her son. As the years moved on finances had become a little easier and she now had no real reason to hold down three jobs but it wasn't something she'd ever admit to. Tired and alone she wouldn't return home again until after eleven and then she would just crawl into bed and shut her godforsaken life away, at least until the next morning.

As usual the following day would pan out exactly as the one before.

"Billy did you hear me or am I talking to myself as usual?"

When he didn't answer for a second time, Jackie grabbed her bag and slammed the door shut without a goodbye. Billy had been listening from behind the closed door and now happy that his mother had gone, he emerged from his bedroom. Searching through the kitchen cupboard he moved several cans and packets of food before he found what he was looking for. His mother kept a half bottle of vodka stashed at the back of the cupboard for what she liked to call emergency's, the only problem was, Jackie seemed to have an emergency most nights. Pouring himself a large measure, Billy

noticed that the level had dropped more than he was happy with. Sighing he made a mental note to get another bottle while he was out. If he didn't top up his mothers supply before she found out he'd been tapping into it then there would be hell to pay.
"Ah sod it!"
Billy poured a little more into his glass and after lighting up another cigarette, walked into the living room. He had a good half an hour before Sally arrived and after sniffing his armpits, decided that he could get away without having a shower.
Flopping down onto the sofa Billy turned on the television and flicked through the channels until he found MTV. Suddenly the room was filled with hard rock and as he stood up to play air guitar, the old man from the flat above began to bang loudly on the floor.
"Turn that bleeding racket down or Ill call the Old Bill."
Billy looked up towards the ceiling and could imagine it caving in at any minute. If that happened his mother would go crazy and he wouldn't hear the last of it for days but Billy wasn't going to be told what to do by anyone let alone a pensioner.
"Fuck off you old git!"
Billy Jacobs didn't care that the man was disabled and hardly left the house. He didn't care that at eighty years old the man deserved some peace and quiet, all Billy cared about was having a good time.

Reaching for the remote he turned the volume up so high that the banging and shouting was instantly drowned out. Now oblivious to the complaining Billy shook his head so that his hair flew out to the rhythm of the music.

Sally Durrant climbed the stairs to her boyfriends flat. She hated this part of Hackney it was very rough and the streets always had gangs milling about which scared her. Her father was a cabbie in the city and worked long hours so she didn't get to see him that much. Her mother Audrey, a classroom assistant at the infant school over on Morning Lane, was out for much of the day so when she wasn't at college Sally was left to her own devises. Her parent's dislike of Billy was intense and she was never allowed to bring him home, so there was no alternative but to come over to Ellingfort Road. As she approached the front door, Sally smiled when she heard the music blearing out. Just as she was about to knock on the door, Albert Morley from the flat above, leant over the balcony and called out to her.

"Oi you! Tell that scumbag to turn it down or I'm phoning the Old Bill."

Sally could feel her cheeks redden with embarrassment and she rapped as hard as she could on the door. Luckily there was a lull between tracks and Billy had heard her.

"Hi Babe, come on in. Fuck me Sal you don't half look sexy!"

To Billy Jacobs she was a goddess. Tall and slim with the blondest of hair she could have been a model but all Sally Durrant wanted out of life was a family and a place of her own and if she was really lucky, to qualify as a hairdresser. Barging past him she marched into the living room. Billy knew by the look on her face that he was in for an ear bashing.
"Now what have I done?"
"I've just got a mouthful from that old bastard upstairs."
"Fuck him."
Billy Jacobs tried to take her in his arms but Sally roughly pushed him away.
"You have to start taking some responsibility. I think your mums right when she says........"
Billy didn't want to hear what was coming next and cut her off mid sentence. He got this sort of ear ache on a daily basis from his old woman without his girlfriend throwing in her two penneth. Without letting her finish he turned and walked into the hall. Entering the kitchen he poured another measure of the vodka but Sally was soon standing behind him.
"Don't walk away from me when I'm talking to you."
"Then stop bending me bleeding ear all the time. You aint half starting to sound like me old woman."
"Well maybe you should do something about it. Have you ever thought that just maybe Jackie's got a point?"
Billy smirked and his facial expression made Sally

want to punch him.

"I aint kidding Billy, if you don't sort yourself out then were finished."

Again he tried to hug her and again she pushed him away.

"So what am I supposed to do? Oh I know I'll go get a lottery ticket and then well be set up. How's that for sorting myself out?"

"Don't be sarky; I was talking about getting a job."

"Like where? I mean they aint exactly queuing up to offer me anything down the job centre, now are they? Fuck me Sal, what do you expect me to do?"

Sally Durrant poured herself a drink and Billy watched the contents of the bottle diminish even further. It was now imperative that he had to replace it today, that or his mother would really throw a wobbly on him.

Look, your Mum works three jobs, my Mum and Dad work, so you aint got any excuse. When I've finished at college, don't think I'm going to doss about all day because I bleeding well aint. There's a big wide world out there Billy Jacobs and I want some of it. If you are happy to just toss your life away, then there's nothing I can do about that but don't expect me to join you."

"Ok ok! I hear you, now come and give us a kiss. You know I love you don't you?"

As she walked over to him, Billy pointed to his groin.

"Someone else is pleased to see you as well Sal."

Sally Durrant placed her glass on to the worktop before heading into the hall. Turning she smiled in Billy's direction as she spoke.
"Not a chance mate!"
"Oh come on babe pleaseeeeeee!"
"Get a job then maybe you and old woody there will see some action, until then Sally's shop is closed. Got the message?"
With that she walked out of the flat leaving Billy standing with his mouth open. It was the first time she had ever turned him down and he didn't like it. Billy Jacobs was really keen on Sally Durrant and their sex life was or had been, fantastic. Now Billy's only option was a hand job and the idea that it had to be his own hand wasn't appealing. Maybe it really was time to get a job and make something of himself but in all honesty Billy didn't have a clue where to start. Mentally he made another note to pop into the Job Centre again after he'd been to the off-licence but he didn't hold out much hope. The last time he was there, the only thing he was offered from the Muppet behind the counter, was shelf filling at the place where his Mum worked. Then again, beggars couldn't be choosers and if he wanted to get laid in the foreseeable future he had to take whatever was on offer. Turning off the television, he held two fingers up in frustration, not to anyone in particular just to the world in general. Reluctantly Billy pulled on his jacket and headed out of the door. In no hurry to get to the job centre

he walked along slowly and he hadn't got far when he bumped into Lewis Backton. Billy and Light Fingers, as Lewis was known, had been at school together and although not best friends had on occasion hung out when no one else was around.
"Hi there Billy boy, how's it hanging?"
Billy Jacobs smiled at his mate and didn't complain when Light Fingers walked along with him.
"Where you off to?"
"Job centre."
"You fucking traitor! Didn't have you down as one of the working brigade old mate."
"Aint got much choice, Sal's shut up shop till I get a job and works a bit more appealing knowing I'm going to get a little action at the end of the day."
Lewis Backton laughed out loud as he swaggered his walk in an over the top kind of way.
"I'd rather have a wank if it meant not having to work again. Tried it once, never again I can tell you!"
"Why what happened?"
"Well it was about six months after we left school and I wanted some cash for the footie. That was back when I used to go up the Arsenal every other Saturday. Anyway I was walking past Newgents undertakers and there was an advert in the window for a part time pallbearer."
"No!"
"Straight up! Anyway I thought I'd give it a go. Old Newgents wife worked behind the counter, big

old bird who stuffed her face with fucking cream cakes all day. Took a dislike to me right from the start, said I had to smarten myself up. Said to wash me greasy hair and clean under me fucking nails, cheeky bitch!"

"Come on Lew! Hurry up and tell me what happened."

"They sent me to do a funeral after me first couple of hours, now how mad is that? I mean how the fuck was I supposed to know that Newgent, the tight old cunt was really cutting corners? He made the fucking coffins out of really thin ply and you had to handle them like they were me old Nan's best china. Anyway I had my hand on the bottom and started to lift the old codger into the air. I tell you Billy, I couldn't fucking believe it, no word of a lie, me hand went straight through the bottom of the fucking coffin!"

Billy couldn't contain himself and laughed out loud. "Couldn't you hide it?"

"I wish I could have Billy boy but me hand was wedged solid and the wood was nipping me wrist like you wouldn't fucking believe. The more I pulled the more the coffin went from side to side."

"And?"

"Well to cut a long story short the whole lot tipped over and the old boy's corpse rolled out and lay on the floor of the Crem. The family was screaming and old Newgent was giving me daggers. The bastards sacked me there and then and never even

paid me for the two hours work I did for them."
Tears streamed down Billy Jacobs face and he held his stomach with pains of laughter. Lewis couldn't see what was so funny and quickly changed the subject.

"So you're under the fucking thumb now are you?"
Billy's mood changed instantly and he stopped dead in his tracks. He was quickly getting pissed off with people today. What with his Mother, that old bastard from the flat upstairs, Sally laying down the law and now this prick slagging him off he'd just about had a gut full.

"And when was the last time you got a shag?"
"Ok mate, don't get fucking shirty I was only saying."
"Well fucking don't alright?"
"Alright mate calm down! Best you go get a job, then maybe it'll put you in a better mood."

Billy's face was becoming red with anger and Lewis could see that any minute he was going to get a clump if he didn't shut up. Light Fingers stepped back and held up both palms in submission. Deciding that his mate wasn't in the best frame of mind to be around, he said his goodbyes and headed down the next available street. Billy continued along but he was now fed up to the back teeth and felt as though he would explode at any moment. He had intended to go straight to the job centre but decided his first port of call should really be the off licence, if only to keep his mother off his back. Turning into Mentmore Terrace he could feel the first spots of rain. This really was turning into a shit day and he couldn't wait for it to be over.

CHAPTER TWO

As he walked down Mentmore Terrace, Billy couldn't stop himself thinking about Sally and all that she had said. He knew deep down that she was right but he didn't know how to change things. When his mother had informed him that he was in a rut Billy had just rolled his eyes upwards and told her to get out of the way of the telly. Now he understood what she'd meant, though it really went against the grain to have to agree with her. Nodding his head to the numerous young men he knew and who now spent their days hanging around on street corners, Billy Jacobs could see that he was no different from any of them and it bothered him. Turning the corner he spied Johnny Drake and Simon the Specs and knew he would have to stop for a chat, that or they would think he was being funny and then they'd get the hump with him.

"Hi lads how's it going?"

"Pukka Billy thanks"

As Billy Jacobs looked into Johnny Drakes eyes he saw something new. It wasn't the dilated pupils caused by smoking to much weed; Johnny had been a dope head for years now. It wasn't the small scabs that had begun to surround his old friend's mouth and which told Billy that his mate had obviously moved on in the world of drugs. What Billy noticed was the look of someone who had just given up on

life. Given up any kind of hope and had just accepted that this was his life until he died or won the lottery and the latter was about as likely to happen as Michael Jackson making president. As Johnny continued to talk, Billy glanced sideways into the shop window desperate to see if in any way he resembled the two men in front of him.
"Fucking boring you are we?"
Billy now turned to face Specs and was embarrassed that his lack of interest in the conversation hadn't gone unnoticed.
"Sorry Si just a bit of the old vanity you know. Hey man what happened to your fucking bins?"
Simon Thaxter had worn glasses from the time he could walk and every year the lenses had become thicker and thicker. Now they resembled bottle bottoms and when you looked directly into them they were so magnified that they made Simon Thaxter's eyes appear huge and bug like.
"Me old man decided to have a go at me last night but the wanker ended up doing more damage to these than me. I wouldn't mind but they're the only pair I've got."
Simon fingered the large wad of sticking plaster that had been used to hold the frames together in several places. All three men laughed out loud but there and then Billy decided things had to change, if they didn't, then he would end up turning into a clown like the two standing before him. Billy had never really taken much of an interest in drugs while he'd

been growing up. The odd spliff on a rainy afternoon or while at a party had been the sum total of his dabbling but he could see that Johnny and Specs were on a slippery slope and heading towards harder things. The sad thing was they didn't even know it.

"Well Id better be off lads."

"Where you going to Billy boy? Maybe me and old Specs here will keep you company. We aint got much else to do."

Billy knew what would occur if he told them about the Job Centre. The last thing he wanted was a repeat of what had happened a few minutes earlier with Light Fingers and he knew these two would probably pull the piss out of him far worse than Lewis had.

"Nah your alright Johnny I'm only going to the offie to get the old woman a bottle then I'm straight back home."

Johnny Drake slapped Billy on the shoulder and almost propelled him along the pavement.

"Then the offie it is, come on Specs."

Billy Jacobs puffed out his cheeks in annoyance but continued along the road without complaint.

As the three entered Sameer's Mini Mart Billy knew that he had to keep his distance. Although Lewis was the one who was well known in the area for thieving, these two weren't above lifting the odd item if they could get away with it.

Sameer Choudry eyed the three men suspiciously as

they walked down the first isle of his shop. Close circuit television cameras were placed in strategic positions but still the locals seemed to have a knack of being able to steel from him without getting noticed. Sameer kept a safe distance. Challenging them wouldn't be an option, not after the last incident but all the same he didn't take his eyes off the monitor for a second. His face still bore the bruises from two weeks ago when he'd caught two small boys stealing from him and had held onto one of them until the police arrived. A few hours later the guilty culprit had been released without charge and Sameer had received a severe beating from the boy's father. Sometimes he wondered if it was really worth trying to make a living honestly. Maybe it would be better to just take what he wanted like most of the people who used his shop did. When Harry Stanton the local beat bobby walked in for his daily newspaper the look of sheer relief on Sameer's face was clear for all to see.
"Morning Sammy."
Sameer didn't reply which wasn't like him and Harry Stanton followed the shopkeepers eyes as they looked down the aisle and then up to the monitor.
"Trouble?"
"Could be officer, I don't really know yet."
Harry looked up at the television set that doubled as a security monitor and caught a quick glimpse of Johnny Drake slipping a bottle of whisky into his

coat pocket.

"Sammy! Lock the front door."

Doing as he was asked Sameer then placed the key behind the counter.

"Is the back door locked?"

Sameer nodded.

"Right Ill call for back up and well have these little toe rags out of your way before you know it." Harry Stanton switched on his radio and whispered that he needed assistance urgently. His colleges would probably moan when they got here but Harry didn't care. Poor old Sameer had been through the wringer in the last couple of weeks and it was going to stop, at least if Harry had anything to do with it. In less than a minute two more uniformed officers were tapping on the shops front door. About to go on a break, Steve Roberts and Dave Linden had been seated in their patrol car just around the corner from the Mini Mart. After letting the officers in, Sameer made a hasty retreat behind the counter. He couldn't abide confrontation and police or no police, was scared of getting another beating. The three policemen quietly walked down the aisle and stopped directly behind Johnny, Billy and Specs.

"Right then lads what seems to be going on here?" Billy had just picked up a bottle of cheap vodka when he heard the man's voice. For some reason and although he'd done nothing wrong, he panicked and the bottle smashed to the floor. Glass shards scattered everywhere and the vodka splashed several other products that would now have to be thrown away.

"That's it! Dave cuff them and take them in will you."

"On what charge mate?"

"Well that one there has a bottle in his pocket that he had no intention of paying for."

Johnny Drake started to protest but Harry Stanton wasn't listening as he frog marched Johnny to the waiting car.

"Fuck off copper I aint done nothing now get your fucking hands off me!"

"You're really starting to piss me off now Sonny, another word and I'll do you for resisting an arrest"

The threat instantly brought silence and as Billy and Specs were lead out behind their friend, Specs stared in Sameer's direction.

"Fucking Paki bastard!"

Harry sharply turned on Specs.

"Shut it or you'll be done for racial threats as well."

When the place was finally quiet and things had simmered down, Sameer walked to the rear of his shop and began to clear up the broken glass. His nerves couldn't stand much more and he was now worried that the men would come back later for their revenge. After sweeping up the mess Sameer placed the closed sign on the front door and made his way upstairs to the flat above. After this latest little incident he'd finally decided that he couldn't continue struggling anymore. First thing in the morning he would put the shop up for sale. Hopefully it wouldn't take long to sell then he would board the first plane he could and go back home to Pakistan. The tiny flat above his shop on Exmouth Place had once seemed so warm and cosy but as if seeing it for the first time, Sameer noticed how dull and drab it looked. Always too busy for love he'd thrown himself head first into work and now he didn't know why he had even bothered. Over the last twenty years Sameer Choudry had tried really hard to make a success of his business but now alone and defeated he had to at last accept, that there really was nothing left of the great in Great Britain.

At Lower Clapton Road police station, Johnny, Billy and Specs were lead through the back door and into the custody suite. For Johnny and Specs it was a regular scenario but not to Billy. As mouthy as he was to his Mother and even though she assumed he got up to all manner of bad things, he had never had his collar felt until now. Finger prints were taken and then they were all photographed much to the disgust of Johnny Drake but Billy didn't utter a word. When their names and addresses had been logged, the three were placed into individual cells. Harry Stanton had been left to complete the paper work, his colleagues didn't mind missing a cup of tea to help him out but when it came down to form filling he was on his own.

"Were off to the canteen for our break now Harry. You can sort the little buggers out from here."
"Thanks boys."
"You're welcome Harry."
Harry Stanton sighed heavily as he and W.P.C Milldrove, a young rookie he'd borrowed from reception, opened up the cell. Johnny Drake was the first to be dealt with as his case was cut and dry.
"Right out here Sonny."
"I aint your fucking Son copper."
The woman police officer shook her head in a way that told Harry they were all wasters and not worth bothering with. After a short interview Johnny was charged with the theft of a bottle of whisky. Within fifteen minutes and after being informed that he'd be hearing from Highbury Corner Magistrates court in the near future, he was released. Next it was Specs turn and as he hadn't been seen to commit a crime he was cautioned for the use of racial language and released. When it came to Billy officer Stanton saw something different in the lad. It wasn't just the fear and embarrassment, Harry could see that Billy Jacobs was really ashamed of the mess he'd gotten into. Taking him to the same interview room he'd used for Johnny, Harry told Billy to sit down and then informed the W.P.C that she was no longer needed.
"Do us a favour love and get a couple of teas would you?"
"Sugar son?"

"Yes please."

Jackie Milldrove sighed heavily but nodded that she would do as she'd been asked. It didn't bode well not to do favours if you were new at a place but still fetching drinks for local scumbags really went against the grain.

When both men were seated at the table and Billy had stated his name and address for the second time that morning, Harry Stanton surprised his prisoner by turning off the tape recorder.

"So are you going to tell me what all this is about Son?"

Billy Jacobs held his head in his hands but he didn't need any further prompting from the officer. He revealed all about his life and what had happened today. When he reached the part about Sally's ultimatum, Harry couldn't stop himself from laughing.

"It aint funny you know."

"No I'm sure it's not but you youngsters only seem to think about one thing."

"What else is there?"

"Son there is a whole big world out there and you are just throwing away the opportunity to explore it. If I had my time over again Id..."

Billy interrupted before the officer could finish his sentence.

"Oh here we go! You sound just like me old woman."

Harry Stanton took a sip of tea that had been

brought in by W.P.C Milldrove a few minutes earlier.

"Maybe I do, so don't you think it's about time you sat up and took notice? Look when I was your age I wanted it all but there weren't the chances that you now have. The only decent thing available was the force."

"So you're saying I should join up then?"

"No I'm not saying that at all. Look Billy I'm trying to help you here but for some reason you're being really negative."

Billy Jacobs sat up straight in his chair and scratched at his ear in an agitated manner.

"Ok lets go with what you're saying and where do I start in this land of golden opportunity then?"

"At the bottom."

"Shelf stacking is all they've offered me; I suppose I can't get much lower than that."

Harry Stanton suddenly felt annoyed with the boy. If Billy had been called a boy he would have created hell but in Harry eyes and after thirty years on the force that's exactly what William Jacobs was, nothing but a boy.

"And what's wrong with good honest hard work mate. It's not what you do for a living that counts, only how well you do it and the sense of pride that it gives you. No one's saying it's what you have to do for the rest of your life but it's a start. Just think how you'll feel after a hard weeks work and you take home your pay and....."

Billy sighed heavily.

"No I'm being serious here so listen. You get home and have a wash and then you take young Sally out for a nice slap up meal and then, well I don't have to spell it out for you now do I?"

Suddenly Billy grinned. He knew exactly what the man was saying and he liked it.

"Like I said earlier, if I get a job then Sal will let me have my leg over!"

"Well I wouldn't have put it exactly like that and it aint really what I'm trying to get at. Let's look at it another way. Now say you get a job and work hard, where's it going to lead?"

"It could go anywhere, Sal and I could get our own place and......."

"Exactly my point, now let's look at the other scenario. Continue hanging around with those two idiots outside and what's going to happen?"

It wasn't hard for Billy to picture himself in ten years time. Sally would be long gone and his Mother would probably have kicked him out, it was getting pretty close to that already. He could see himself hanging around the estate with Johnny and Specs, he could even see his face covered in sores from glue sniffing or crack taking. Suddenly he knew what he wanted and he smiled at the policeman.

"Thanks mate you've really helped me make me mind up."

Harry Stanton hoped as he always did, that the lad

was speaking the truth and not telling him what he thought Harry wanted to hear.

"Now I suggest you get down that job centre and take the first thing they offer you. Ask for Millicent Abbot and tell her I sent you."

As Billy was lead out of the interview room he suddenly stopped and turned to face Officer Stanton.

"Can I ask a favour?"

"You can ask son but depends what it is."

"Can I go out the back, only those two will be waiting and I can do without the third degree."

Harry smiled. Maybe this time his pep talk, the sort of pep talk that the other officers routinely pulled the piss out of him for, would do some good.

"Of course you can."

Watching Billy walk through the back yard and out of the rear gate made Harry, for a second and only that, consider going out to the front and telling Johnny and Specs that their friend had already left. Smiling to himself he instead headed in the direction of the canteen, it wouldn't hurt the thieving little sods to wait for an hour or two.

CHAPTER THREE

Millicent Abbott had worked at Goswell Road Job Centre in Clerkenwell for the last ten years. Originally she'd had hopes of finding work for everyone that walked through the door but in just a few months her dreams had diminished when she'd daily come up against the long line of no hopers. With no intention of working and only attending the centre so that their benefits wouldn't be cut, to Millicent they were a total waste of time. Of course, there was the odd person that she had been able to help and occasionally they had even returned to thank her but they were few and far between. No, Millicent Abbot now accepted that it was a thankless task and she was only here for the monthly pay packets that just about kept her and her cat Mr Dobby out of the grasp of poverty.
The centre was run down and until Millicent had decided to impose her own cigarette ban, had stunk to high heavens every day. Most of the job centre users had complained bitterly but after a few stern looks from Millicent, they had reluctantly stubbed out their cigarettes. It was six months earlier when she had begun to enforce things and Millicent now had a zero tolerance policy to anyone lighting up in her place of work. Millicent Abbot had met Harry Stanton quite by chance when he had popped in to check up on another young lad that he had taken under his wing. Now they had a special friendship,

a friendship that was swiftly deepening as together they tried to clean up the area. They both knew in reality it was a hopeless task but it wouldn't stop them trying. It was on one of their weekly meetings down at the Red Lion pub; too of course discuss their tactics but which Millicent saw as a date, that Harry had first put forward his proposal. If he came across a genuine case, where someone really wanted to change their lives, he would send them to her. Every few weeks a respectable vacancy would come into the office and Millicent would hold it back for as long as possible, in the hope that Harry would send someone over.

One such situation had arisen and that's how Billy Jacobs found himself sitting opposite the chubby woman who wore her spectacles on the tip of her nose. Millicent Abbott's desk was neat and tidy and everything had its place but Billy couldn't help but laugh at the furry animals that were dotted around her computer. Fluffy Gonk's like the toys little girls had at infant school were stuck with suction pads to the top and sides of the screen.

"Something funny young man?"

"No not really and I'm sorry for laughing."

Millicent Abbott coughed into her hand as she pushed her glasses back onto the bridge of her nose and looked Billy up and down.

"If its benefits you've come about, you've got the wrong department."

"No its nothing to do with benefits. I'm just here

because Officer Stanton sent me and he said to ask for you special like."

Billy could visibly see the woman's chest swell and for a second he grinned at the image of old Stanton feeling her up in the store cupboard after the place closed for the day. When the woman again coughed, he wiped the smile from his face and tried to appear serious.

"Well if Harry, I mean Officer Stanton sent you then I will do my best to help. Now what kind of work have you done in the past?"

For a moment Billy was embarrassed by her question but he knew, just like the policeman had said, he had to start at the bottom.

"Bit of a problem there see, I aint actually worked before but don't think I'm lazy because I aint. Officer Stanton told me I had to be prepared to start at the bottom and I'll take anything you've got."

For the first time Millicent Abbott smiled. She liked the look of this lad and after all, even though her professional standards may have slipped a little recently, she was here to help people and of course pleasing Harry as well would be a bonus.

"I don't think you'll have to start at the bottom young man. Now as luck would have it, a very good vacancy came in this morning."

Billy's ears pricked up as he imagined all sorts of work, it might even be something in the city. Now that would really impress Sal.

"Green Lawns Manor need a care assistant. The pay

is above the minimum wage and they are prepared to train the successful candidate to the guideline levels required. Of course you'll have to smarten yourself up a bit. Now would you like me to arrange an interview for tomorrow?"
Suddenly Billy's dreams came crashing down around his ears.
"Green Lawns Manor, what's that?"
Millicent Abbott inhaled deeply and rubbed her hands together. She always liked it when she had to detail a job; it somehow made her feel superior.
"Well, it's a nursing care home over on Gore Road. It only takes residents who are suffering from dementia and the likes. It's a very responsible position I might add, hence the higher rate of pay."
"Fucking dementia!"
"I beg your pardon young man but I, we, do not tolerate swearing and bad behaviour at this Job Centre. Now if you're not interested in the position then just say so but please do not sit there and abuse me or waste my time."
Billy couldn't believe what was being offered to him and for a second he eyed the man with suspicion, was the copper taking the piss out of him. He knew that if he walked out now, then that was his future over and he might as well kiss goodbye to Sally and any hope of a sex life in the foreseeable future. Deciding that he should give it a go, if he only lasted a week then at least he would get some spare cash, he smiled at the woman.

"I'm sorry. It's just that I hadn't even considered that kind of work."
Millicent tapped at her lips with her index finger. She could ask the young man to leave but then she didn't want to let Harry down and besides care homes always needed new blood and just maybe the boy would turn out to be good at it.
"Apology accepted. Now wait there and I will phone ahead for an interview time. Oh and don't think about pinching any of my little friends because I know exactly how many I have and I will instantly know if you've taken one of them." He wanted to burst out laughing at her words but managed to keep a straight face. Waiting for her to come back, Billy began to have second thoughts as images of mental asylums that he'd seen in films entered his mind. Sitting opposite Millicent's funny little desk, it was several minutes later before she returned and when she did, Millicent could clearly see that the entire colour had drained from her clients face.
"Are you feeling alright?"
"Yeah I'm fine."
"Right then, they will see you tomorrow morning at ten sharp and remember to smarten yourself up. Here is the address and the name of the person you need to ask for and please do be punctual!"
Billy took the introduction card from her chubby hand and headed towards the door.
"Mr Jacobs! It really isn't a bad place you know; my

own Mother was a resident there for a while."
"I'll take your word for it Missus, bye."
Billy pushed the card into his pocket as he exited the centre and began a slow walk home. He prayed that he wouldn't bump into Johnny or Specs because he didn't have a clue how he would explain about this job but then again he reasoned that it probably wouldn't come to anything. Billy chuckled to himself but deep down he now wanted to work and if his friends thought he was a prat then that was their problem.

The following morning saw William Jacobs up by seven am. As usual his Mother had left at six but before she went, had laid out a clean white shirt for him. The previous night and an hour before she'd begun her shift at the cinema, her son had surprised her by chatting to her as she prepared their dinner. When he'd asked her to press a shirt for him, Jackie Lemon was shocked but she hadn't let it show, she just hoped with all her heart that her son was finally turning his life around.

After making himself some toast and a cup of tea Billy dressed in the darkest jeans he could dig out of his wardrobe. Examining his reflection in the mirror he wondered if he should wear a tie but after searching through his chest, was only able to come up with the old one he'd worn for school, so he decided against it. It was now twenty four hours since he'd heard from Sally and it had taken all his will power not to phone her. There wouldn't have been any point, he hadn't got the job yet and she would have only hung up on him.

The directions Millicent Abbott had written on the card were clear and precise and Billy found Green Lawns Manor in less than twenty minutes. Approaching the building that had originally been four large houses but had long since been converted into one, he was disappointed. Stupidly he'd imagined a real manor house with rolling expanses of grass and large gardens but in hindsight that would have been a near impossibility in this area of the smoke. Ringing the bell, he waited nervously to be let in and when he saw someone approach through the toughened glass door, he coughed and stood up straight. The door didn't open and all he heard was someone on the other side say Who is it? Billy said his name and again the voice said Who is it? Again he repeated his details but when he was asked Who is it for the third time he started to get frustrated. Deciding to ring the bell once more, he stood back and waited. A second figure moved in the direction of the door and then the silhouette of two people struggling could be seen. Billy's eyes opened wide in fear and from the inside he heard someone begin to shout.

"Edna! Get away from there; you know you're not allowed near the front door!"

"Who is it?"

"Edna! If I have to tell you again you can go to your room."

Suddenly all manner of bolts could be heard sliding and unlocking and at last the door was opened by a tall woman in a white uniform.

"Sorry about that love but our Edna can be a handful at times. Please come in."

Billy Jacobs sheepishly stepped inside imagining he was going to see something horrendous. What greeted him was a large hallway lit by several lamps and which gave the place a warm glow.

"Now how can I help you?" "I'm here about the job."

"Right, well follow me and I'll take you to Mrs Dewey's office."

The woman, who Billy would later come to know as Wendy Saxby, marched ahead and he had to widen his stride to keep up with her. Tall and slim, Wendy wore her dark hair very short and for a moment it crossed Billy's mind that she might be queer. A slight smile began to appear at the corners of his mouth as he imagined her in a passionate clinch with another woman. Suddenly he stopped daydreaming; if she got her kicks by doing a bit of rug munching then it wasn't any of his business. Billy silently chastised himself, he really had to get Sally on side or he would blow his top, this sex ban was a lot harder than he could have imagined.

A few of the residents were milling around, some with Zimmer frames and others just with, as Billy called them, old people sticks. A man dressed only in pyjamas waltzed along the hall with an invisible partner. Wendy gave a little smile when she saw the look of alarm on the boys face. Touching Billy's arm she gave him a friendly wink.

"It's really not as bad as it looks. Some of them are real sweethearts and if you get the job you'll soon find out which are the ones to avoid."

Billy gulped hard as Wendy pushed open the door and held out her hand, silently indicating for him to go inside.

"Hello there! You must be William, please take a seat."

Isobel Dewey was small in stature and her navy two piece was stretched tight at the seams. Plump and with the style of perm that went out in the seventies, she reminded Billy of a teacher back in his school days. Shaking the woman's hand Billy then took a seat in the chair opposite her.

"Now tell me all about yourself William."

Billy relayed all that his mother and Sally had said, minus the sex ban and the time spent in Officer Stanton's company. He explained that his life didn't seem to be going anywhere and he desperately needed a job.

"Well William..."

"Most people call me Billy."

"Well Billy, I have to be honest. You're not exactly what were looking for but we are extremely short staffed at the moment. So if you're willing to give it a go then there is a position here for you if you want it, on a three month trial of course."

You mean I've got the job Mrs Dewey?"
"I do indeed and if you could start tomorrow that would be great. Now I'm not going to sugar coat things and tell you it's wonderful here because it isn't. It can be very demanding and at times stressful but if you work hard, then I think you will be surprised at just how rewarding it can be. Oh and Billy we don't stand on ceremony around here there just isn't the time. Everyone's on first name terms including me. From now on call me Isobel or as the residents like to refer to me, Izzy. Now if you'd like to go and find Wendy, shell sort you out with a uniform and explain the work rotas."
Izzy glanced at the dial of her oversized watch.
"I should think she'll be in the dining room about now, probably starting to prepare elevenses for the residents."
Walking into the hallway he passed Edna who this time was none to friendly. Smiling in her direction, Billy was shocked when she spat at him and the offending phlegm landed at his feet. Right at this moment nothing could dampen his spirits, not even this old fruitcake. The man dressed in pyjamas was still waltzing up and down the hall but the sight now made Billy only want to laugh. He thought back to yesterday when he'd been with Johnny and Specs and how crazy everything had been. In the grand scale of things, this place now didn't seem that different, just crazy in a different sort of way.
After collecting his crisp white tunic Billy began his

journey home. The walk was completed in record time and his thoughts were filled with just how lucky he was.

Jackie Lemon was seated at the kitchen table when he walked in. Rolling her eyes upwards she knew that her relaxation time was about to come to an abrupt halt. Unusually, Billy placed the kettle on the stove and asked his mother if she'd like a fresh cup of tea. For a moment she stared open mouthed wondering if her real son had been abducted by aliens. When he told her about the job Billy didn't expect the reaction his mother gave. Jumping up from the table she flung her arms around his neck and held on for dear life.

"Alright Mum there's no need to go over the bleeding top, it aint like I'm going to be a brain surgeon or anything."

"Son, it's as good as, to me anyway. I tell you what why don't you phone young Sally up and ask her to come over later? I'll call in sick tonight at the cinema then Ill cook us all a nice meal to celebrate. I've got some vodka in the cupboard and after we can have a few drinks, what do you say?"

Billy glanced in the direction of the cupboard as the realisation that he hadn't replaced the bottle hit home. With all that had gone on yesterday it had completely slipped his mind. Turning to face her Billy smiled.

"That would be lovely Mum, thanks."

As Jackie Lemon slipped on her coat and left the flat

for a lunchtime stint at the supermarket Billy dialled Sally's number. He already knew what was on the cards when he told Sally all that had happened and he couldn't wait for her to come round.

"Hi babe! Now don't hang up I've got something to tell you. You'll be pleased to hear that I've got a job and start tomorrow."

"Oh Billy, that's brilliant news."

"My Mum wants to cook us dinner tonight to celebrate so will you come over?"

"Yeah of course I will, what time?"

"Well I was thinking more like now, I mean we have a little problem to sort out if I remember rightly."

On the other end of the line Sally Durrant could be heard giggling loudly.

"Oh and Sal? Bring a half bottle of vodka round will you?"

Hanging up Billy made his way into the bedroom to change and to check that the bed was in a reasonable state for his girlfriend. Sitting down he recalled all that had happened this morning and a wide grin suddenly spread across his face. It was strange but as excited as he was to be seeing Sally, Billy Jacobs was even more excited at the thought of starting work the next day.

CHAPTER FOUR

Up, even before his Mother, Billy had fresh tea made and was merrily placing bread in the toaster when Jackie Lemon entered the kitchen. The radio was switched on low and Billy swayed his hips to the music as he prepared breakfast. She really couldn't believe the transformation in her son and just prayed it would last. The three of them had enjoyed a lovely evening the previous night but now in the cold light of day she wondered if her Billy would last until the end of his shift. Still she wouldn't dampen his spirits by letting him know her thoughts. It had been such a long time since she'd actually enjoyed her sons company and she wanted to savour it for as long as possible.
"Morning Son, sleep well?"
"Yeah I really did and thanks again for last night Mum it was cracking. Now I've made you some toast but I have to get off now as me shift starts at seven."
"Why so early?"
Billy picked up his jacket from the back of the chair. "I've got to get the oldies ready for their breakfast. Now I should be back around four. Oh and Mum don't worry about tea tonight. Ill pop down the chippie and get us both a nice piece of cod."
As Jackie Lemon watched her only child leave the flat a tear trickled down her cheek. He looked so smart in his crisp white uniform and at last she

would have something to brag about to the girls at the supermarket.

From the outside Green Lawns Manor looked just as drab and uninviting as it had yesterday but nothing could lower Billy's spirits. He was getting on well with his Mum; he had a beautiful girlfriend and now a job, what could possibly go wrong.

Ringing the bell and waiting to be let in, he half expected the scenario of yesterday to begin but Edna was nowhere in sight.

A few minutes later and after Billy had started to worry that he'd dreamt the whole job thing, Wendy Saxby at last opened the door.

"Sorry about that darling but it's like a bleeding mad house here in the mornings. I must say I think they've chucked you in at the deep end."

"Why?"

"This shift is the worse there is. After a long night in bed a lot of the old buggers are real grumpy, not to mention the fact that they can get a bit violent but then that's why we have Lawrence here. Oh you aint met him yet have you, well you will in a minute. Now come with me and I'll show you where to hang your coat then wed best get on with it before they start screaming blue murder."

After Billy had put his things away he followed Wendy upstairs where they were met out on the landing by a tall thickset man of African origin.

"Here he is! Billy this is Lawrence Smith. Lawrence this is Billy Jacobs our newest recruit."

The men shook hands and Billy was mesmerised at the size of Lawrence, his hand entirely covered Billy's and the fact that Lawrence stood over six feet six inches tall and looked down on Billy, didn't make him feel very comfortable.

"Very pleased to make your acquaintance Son. Now then Wendy, I've put Granny Davis in the dining room. George and Dulcie are happy to make their own way down so that just leaves Ruby and Edna."

"Fair enough, you take Edna and we'll see to Ruby." Walking into the room at the end of the corridor Billy was surprised to see a little old lady standing in her nightdress and staring out of the window. She looked so tiny and ill offensive and Billy couldn't think why it needed two people to get her ready.

"Morning Ruby love, ready for some food? Now this is our new member of staff, his name is Billy. Billy this is Ruby Fulcher."

The woman didn't reply and just continued to stare out of the window. Wendy removed a top and trousers from the cupboard and handed them to Billy.

"Right when I say go, you take her nightdress off and try and put the jumper on. At the same time I'll start to do the bottom half."

Wendy Saxby smiled and shook her head when she saw the look of confusion on her assistants face.

"You're wondering why it takes two aren't you."

Billy nodded.

"Right just this once I'll show you, after that you'll do everything as I say without question and things will run smoothly."

Wendy grabbed the clothes and made her way across the room to where Ruby still stood. With one swift movement she raised and removed the woman's nightwear but that was where easy stopped and difficult began. Wendy pulled the jumper over Ruby's head and after quickly pushing her arms through the holes, knelt down and began to pull her trousers on. She hadn't got them up to the woman's knees when Billy noticed Ruby, in record speed, pull the jumper off over her head. When Wendy at last managed to pull the trousers up to Ruby's waist and again pull the jumper over the old woman's head, Ruby had somehow managed to wriggle so that the trousers fell to the floor.

"And so it goes on, now can you see why it takes two to dress the little old bugger?"

Billy wanted to laugh, he'd never seen anything so comical well not unless it was on the telly and even then he hadn't believed that things like that really happened.

"Now you grab the jumper and when I say go don't stop till she's dressed. Heaven help us!

At this rate shell still be eating her bloody breakfast at lunch time."

As Billy pulled the jumper down over Ruby's head

he suddenly felt a pain in his arm and pulled away sharply.

"She's just nipped me bleeding arm!"

Wendy laughed out loud, he really did have a lot to learn and the quicker he picked things up then the fewer bruises he would find at the end of the day.

"I meant to warn you about that, she likes to nip does our Ruby and she aint against giving the odd bite if she can get away with it. You'll soon learn to have eyes up your arse in this place darling."

Somehow Billy and Wendy managed to accomplish the task and were about to lead Ruby out onto the landing when the door flew open and Edna O'Brien burst in, followed in hot pursuit by Lawrence. Waving her arms wildly in the air Billy grimaced at the smell which now filled the room.

"Chocolate chocolate, I've got chocolate!"

Diving forward, Edna roughly rubbed her hands all over Ruby's face.

"Oh fuck Lawrence weren't you watching her?. Now we've got to bleeding start all over again. Billy! Go into the bathroom and warm the shower up. Izzy's due on in a minute and if these two are covered in shit she's going to do her bleeding nut."

Ruby began to scream at the top of her voice and the other residents who were on the landing and about to make their way down to breakfast, started to join in. Seconds later and the whole place was in chaos.

"Bloody hell this is all I need!"

Billy Jacobs just stood with his mouth wide open.
"Billy did you hear me? Go and put the shower on so we can get them both cleaned up."
Thirty minutes later and both Ruby and Edna had been washed and changed and were now sitting in the dining room with the other residents, smiling as if nothing had ever happened. The long table could seat twelve people, though today it only contained five. Recently a few residents had passed away and as yet their places at Green Lawns hadn't been filled. Billy was grateful for that fact, it was hard enough with just five but another seven to look after didn't bare thinking about. Wendy Saxby emerged with a tray of teas but they weren't in china cups. Each drink was sealed in a plastic beaker like the ones given to children.
"Right Billy hand these out while I go and get the food. I know it's not very nice in theses but believe me, a face full of shits a lot easier to deal with than scolding hot tea."
Out of nowhere a timid little voice could be heard asking Is it dinner time yet, is it dinner yet, where's me dinner?
Turning round he saw the tiniest woman he had ever seen sitting in a special type of high chair. The woman must have been a hundred is she was a day and the sight had Billy mesmerised. Wendy came back into the dining room and kneeling down beside the chair, placed a bowl onto the floor and began loading a spoon with the mushy contents that

didn't resemble any particular type of food.

"Alright Granny, it's now coming love."

Billy would soon learn all the residents names and habits and the first would be Granny Davis. Aged one hundred and two she was the oldest occupant of Green Lawns. Her only interest in life was food and with an inbuilt alarm she would ask the same question over and over again every meal time. It was the only words she ever spoke and putting her frail condition aside, she seemed to be the easiest of the five to care for. George Martin, the only male living at the home was the one Billy had seen yesterday dancing with his invisible partner. George had served in the war and liked everything carried out with military precision. On the odd occasion when he wasn't dancing and had decided to be naughty, he could be swiftly brought into line by Lawrence. Pretending to be an army officer, Lawrence Smith would bark orders and George would obey his command instantly.

Edna O'Brien as Billy had quickly found out, was the trouble maker and worse behaved out of them all. She could be violent but that wasn't her only bad habit. Edna had a fixation, as Billy had been witness to earlier, with faeces. For some reason she really believed that shit was chocolate and it caused huge work problems on a daily basis. Edna had to be watched like a hawk and at the first signs of her beginning to strain; she would be frogmarched to the toilet as quickly as possible. Ruby Fulcher who

Billy had helped to dress was mostly quiet and apart from her little bouts of nipping and biting was relatively well behaved. The last person sitting at the table was introduced as Dulcie Grey. At only sixty three years of age she was one of the youngest residents in Green Lawns and spent much of her time alone in her room. Wendy Saxby couldn't really tell Billy much about the woman apart from the fact that she'd been here a little over five years and didn't speak much.
"So is this how it is every meal time?"
"No this is a good day."
Wendy fed another spoonful of mush into Granny's mouth which was constantly opening and closing like a bird.
"If they were all like her it would be a doddle to work here. Now Billy, hand round those bowls of cereal and watch they don't choke. After that you can finish off here if you like but take your time and don't let her get hold of the spoon because she misses her mouth more times than she manages it."
Finally by ten o'clock breakfast had at last been served. The residents were now all seated in the lounge watching television and Billy helped Wendy to take the dishes into the kitchen.
"Make us all a cuppa love while I rinse these out. It'll be quiet for a while, now that they've all been fed and watered."
Billy Jacobs did as he was asked and walking back into the dining room placed the three mugs onto the

table. A few seconds later he was joined by Wendy and Lawrence.

"Well what do you think to it so far then Billy?"

Billy puffed out his cheeks as he thought of how to answer.

"Well it aint exactly what I imagined. I aint saying I don't like it but getting faced with a woman covered in shit on your fist day aint exactly endearing me to the place I can tell you."

Wendy looked at Lawrence and they both burst out laughing at the same time. Wendy Saxby had seen many young people come and go in her time at Green Lawns. Some lasted a few days and some only a few hours but she had a good feeling about this latest recruit.

Billy had been back at the flat for a couple of hours when his mother returned from her shift at the supermarket. He'd changed out of his whites and now sat watching television as he always did. Placing her key in the lock Jackie Lemon heard the music blearing out and rolled her eyes upwards. About to shout at her son to turn it down, she was more than a little surprised when he switched off the television and emerged from the living room.

"Here, let me give you a hand with those."

Billy took the two bags of groceries from his mother and walked into the kitchen.

"I'll make us both a cuppa then nip and get the fish and chips. You look done in Mum; don't you think it's about time you gave up at least one of them jobs?"

Jackie Lemon sat at the table and while her son proceeded to put the shopping away she slipped off her shoes and rubbed at her tired feet.

"Maybe I should think about it but enough about me for now. How'd you get on today love?"

Billy told his mother all that happened and when he reached the part where Edna had smeared Ruby with shit, Jackie almost wretched.

"I tell you this for nothing Son, there's no way I could clean them up. I'm right proud of you, truly I am."

Billy smiled at his mother's comment but he also smiled for himself. If someone had told him a few days ago that this was what he would be doing he wouldn't have believed them.

"So will you be going again tomorrow?"

"Going again? of course I will it's me job now."

Jackie couldn't believe the transformation and as doubtful as she'd been this morning she had now changed her mind. It looked like her son had a future at long last; maybe she really would consider giving up one of her jobs. Telling old Timpson to shove his poxy shift where the sun doesn't shine would give her great pleasure.

"You taking Sally out tonight?"

"Nah I aint got no cash till I get paid."

Jackie opened her purse and removed a twenty pound note.

"Here, the pair of you can have a drink on me."

"Thanks Mum but I aint taking your money."
"Well wonders will never bloody cease. Look I want you to have it and you can pay me back when you get your first weeks wages all right? Darling I've waited years to see you get a job and be happy, now just enjoy it alright?"
Billy kissed his Mother tenderly on the cheek and went into the other room to phone his girlfriend. His mother was right, he could pay her back and having his own money was a new feeling for Billy Jacobs, a feeling he really liked. Harry Stanton really did know what he was talking about and Billy was glad that he'd listened to the man.

CHAPTER FIVE

Over the next three months Billy had become really adept at dealing with the residents and none more so than Edna O'Brien. So skilled at spotting when the woman was ready to have one of her episodes, he'd been put in charge of what Wendy liked to call Edna's shit rota. Mrs Dewey was very impressed with her young recruit and thanked his hard work by giving Billy permanent employment. Over the moon, Billy had even begun talking to Sally about getting their own place. At first she had been reluctant but the more she thought about it, the more she started to warm to the idea. When the weather was cold and it was dark outside, they were stuck in Jackie's flat watching television and it was always what Jackie wanted to watch. A place of their own seemed really appealing and she couldn't wait for it to happen. By the time Billy Jacobs got home from the late shift it was just past ten at night. Sally had been keeping Jackie company for the evening but she was relieved when he walked through the door. There were only so many cooking programmes and soaps a young girl could stomach and tonight Sally Durrant had received more than her fare share.
"Hi babe. Been here long?"
Sally rolled her eyes upwards which straight away told Billy that his girlfriend was fed up to her back

teeth.

"Come in the kitchen Sal, I've got something to show you."

Sally giggled but was silenced by a disapproving cough from Jackie. She didn't like smut in any form and hated it when Billy started with his rude innuendos.

"Mum I wasn't being rude you know. Come on Sal, I really have got something to show you."

Sally got up from the sofa but didn't look Jackie in the eye. She knew that if she did she would receive a black look and she was starting to get really fed up with Jackie's disapproving glares. It was like the woman thought they had nothing but sex on their minds and Sally wouldn't have minded that so much but she hadn't had any for over a week now. What with Billy's ever changing shifts and now that his mother had given up her evening job, it always seemed to be the three of them and they never got any alone time. In some ways Jackie could be really liberal but where sex was concerned it was a taboo subject. If Billy's mum was in residence then his bedroom was strictly off limits.

Alone in the kitchen Sally waited for a present or something but when Billy handed her a pile of papers she frowned.

"What's this?"

"Me lunch break was at four today so I was able to pop out and catch the estate agents just before they closed. A lot of them are well out of our price range but there is a couple of flats over Bethnal Green way that we could just about afford."

Sally studied the top two details and tuned her nose up. Even from the photographs they all appeared really small and when she read the monthly rent she gasped out loud.

"Billy that's ridiculous we could never afford any of these places, not even when I'm qualified and we've got two wages coming in."

"Now don't just dismiss it without hearing me out. Izzy called me into the office today and guess what?"

"Oh I don't know Billy, just spit it out will you. It really pisses me off when you start with the guessing games."

For a moment he wondered if this really was the best time to be talking about moving in together. For some reason Sally was agitated and Billy knew that when she was like this, everything he said would be wrong.

"Look would you rather leave this till tomorrow? I don't mind really but if we end up arguing then I'd rather not..."

Sally Durrant stood up and before Billy had finished speaking she planted a kiss on her boyfriend's cheek.

"I'm sorry and no let's talk now. Anything's better than having to watch telly with your mum, it's almost driven me up the bleeding wall tonight but I shouldn't take it out on you. Now what did Izzy want?"

"She's only gone and upped me wages and not by a little I can tell you. She said that I had settled in really well and that she didn't want to lose me, so I now get the same rate of pay as the others. Seems the low wages was only to see if Id stick at it, now I've proved myself and they've made me permanent, then the moneys going to reflect that."

"That's great but these two flats don't look so good babe. I know we want a place of our own but it's still got to be somewhere fit for human habitation." Billy wrapped his arms around her and Sally willingly nestled her head against his chest.

"There's no harm in taking a butchers, now is there? I don't start me shift till two tomorrow and I know you aint got college so I made a couple of appointments."

"Well I suppose it won't hurt to have a look, now are you going to walk me home?"

Grabbing their coats the couple said a hasty farewell to Jackie before disappearing out of the front door. Albert Morley from the flat upstairs, was leaning over the balcony as Billy and Sally left. Glancing up, Billy spotted the old man and nodded his head, the gesture was returned but it seemed awkward. Since getting a job the young man had stopped playing that mind numbing music at a deafening volume and it was something Albert Morley was grateful for. He couldn't bring himself to actually speak to the boy but at the same time he wanted to keep civil, just in case young Billy Jacobs found himself out of work. If that happened, at least he would be able to knock on the door without the fear of being punched or even worse. As the couple disappeared down the stairwell Albert Morley shook his head, the youth of today were nothing but worthless yobs. Now it was different in his day, in his day older people commanded and received respect. Today pensioners just seemed to be a nuisance to the rest of society and Albert Morley hated being a nuisance to anyone. One day the younger generation would find out what it was like to be old and not wanted and that thought brought a smile to Albert's face. It was just a pity he wouldn't be around when Billy was old and some young kid was winding him up with loud music all the time.

The next morning Billy was up and about far earlier than was needed. His mother had already left for her morning cleaning shift and he mooched around the flat willing time to pass quickly. At nine o'clock he was so excited that he couldn't wait around another minute. He'd agreed to meet Sally at ten outside the first property on the list. Billy worked out that if he walked slowly he could stretch the journey out for half an hour. The rest of the time he could spend having a good look round the outside of the building. Strolling along he hadn't got far when in the distance he spied Johnny Drake and Si the Specs. Not wanting a repeat of a few months

ago he just held up his hand in acknowledgment before turning onto Wilton Way. It wasn't on his rout but it was still better than getting into a conversation with Johnny and Specs. Billy was well aware that they would want to tag a long and that Sal would blow her stack if she saw her boyfriend with those two no hopers. He daydreamed as he walked along and at first didn't hear the voice call out to him. It took Officer Stanton a second attempt before Billy stopped and looked across the road. In the past he would just have ignored the man but not now, now Billy was happy to see the one person who had helped him turn his life around. Crossing the road his face beamed as he approached the policeman.
"Hello there Billy lad and how's things with you?"
"Couldn't be better thanks and I owe you big time for helping me get that job."
"You're welcome. Now how's that girlfriend of yours? I can see by the smile on your face that the two of you have made up your differences."
Billy grinned as he remembered telling the policeman about Sal's sex ban.
"She fine thanks. I'm off to meet her now actually, going to look at a couple of flats."
"Are you now, well that's good news."
"They made me permanent yesterday so my moneys gone up and when you take on the responsibility of your own place you have to make sure that you can cover your bills."

"You do indeed Billy and it's nice to see you doing so well. Now take care and if you need any help then come and find me."

"I will and thanks again Officer Stanton."

As Billy walked away Harry Stanton couldn't help but smile. It felt good to know that at least one misguided youngster hadn't fell through the net and this one was coming on in leaps and bounds. Tonight he was meeting up with Millicent and he couldn't wait to tell her all about Billy Jacobs and how things had turned out.

The house on Globe Road was the second in a row of a Victorian terrace which had been divided into three flats. Walking around to the rear of the property Billy opened the back gate. The small yard was filled with black bin liners that were overflowing with household rubbish. The sight didn't put Billy off, rubbish could soon be got rid of but he still made a mental note not to bring Sally round the back. As he made his way to the front door of the house he could see his girlfriend sitting on the low wall outside the property.

"Hi babe! excited?"

"A bit I suppose, what time can we have a look?"

"The geezer said he'd meet us here at ten, I think that's him now coming."

Alistair Weston had worked as an estate agent for just over a year and he'd hated every second of that time. Aware from the beginning that Woodley and Mitch were a down market agency, even he'd been surprised at how low they could sink. Charging extortionate rents and dealing with scumbag landlords was one thing but the state of most of the rental properties on their books was little short of disgusting. Still he couldn't voice his opinion as he needed the job, so putting on his fake smile he approached his young potential clients.

"Alistair Weston. Pleased to meet you both. Now we need to get a move on as there are several other people already interested in the flat. If you'd like to follow me well get inside and I'll show you both around."

The building had a unit on each level and the details Billy had been given were for the flat on the second floor. As Sally stepped inside she instantly wrinkled her nose at the stale smell. The hallway carpet was matted and sticky and she didn't want to think what the large brown stains were. Squeezing by an abandoned bicycle frame and a discarded rusty pushchair the three made their way up two flights of stairs. After Alistair Weston had struggled for a few seconds trying to unlock the door it at last flew open. The sight which greeted them on the other side was dismal. The small room housed an old bed at one end and a couple of kitchen units at the other. Doors were hanging off and the sink was filled with used tea bags and food wrappers.

"Well if you'd like to follow me I'll show you the bathroom."

"I don't think that's going to be necessary. Billy I

aint staying here, it aint fit for a bleeding dog to live in."

"Hold on Sal it aint that bad. I know it needs a lick of paint here and there but we could soon have it looking nice."

"Nice! You're having a fucking laugh aint you! There's no way in a million years Id ever live in a place like this."

Turning towards Alistair Weston her face was red with rage.

"And you should be ashamed of yourself even advertising something like this is a shit hole. Now let's go and look at the second one and I just hope for your sake that's it's a lot better than this one."

Alistair Weston did feel ashamed and he wanted to tell the young couple that they were wasting their time. The only trouble was he knew that if he did, then word might get back to his boss and he'd be out on his ear. Leading them to his car he didn't have the guts to tell them his thoughts and the five minute car journey was taken in silence. The second place was situated in Punderson's Gardens and was a ten storey tower block. As he switched off the engine, Alistair Weston glanced at Sally in the rear view mirror. The look of horror on her face spoke volumes and he suddenly had a sinking feeling. Still he had to act professional and after locking the car and silently offering up a prayer that he still had four wheels when he returned, he led them inside. The lift was out of order and when he

heard Sally groan out loud he turned to face her.
"Look I shouldn't say anything but in all honesty you're wasting your time. This place is worse than the first one I showed you."
Sally Durrant was now really angry and her words came out with venom.
"Then why the fuck do you keep showing them to people?"
Alistair Weston hung his head in shame as he spoke.
"Fifteen months ago I lost my job in the city. My wife was expecting our first child and we were forced to move in with her overbearing parents. Please don't say anything to Woodley and Mitch because if they found out Id put you off, then I will be shown the door. I've got a wife and child to support!"
Sally instantly felt sorry for the man, how could she have read things so wrong. There she was thinking he was just after their money and he was in a more desperate situation than they were.
"Don't worry our lips are sealed. You get off; well make our own way back."
As Alistair Weston walked out of the building Sally called out Good Luck but there was no reply from the man, a man who looked truly broken. As Billy turned to face his girlfriend he could see that she had tears in her eyes.
"Come on babe it aint the end of the world."
"Aint it? If this is the sum total of what we can

afford then all we've got to look forward to is endless nights of sitting in with your mum."
"Look it might take a bit longer than I thought but I'll take on any extra hours I can get and we'll just have to save a bit harder."
"Oh Billy, I do love you."
Sally Durrant truly loved Billy Jacobs and right at this minute there was no one she'd rather plan her future with, even if it meant her dreams were going to take a little longer to come to fruition than she'd hoped.

CHAPTER SIX

Over the following few days Billy Jacobs wasn't his usual happy self, not that anyone had noticed. His colleagues were all too busy with their work as three new residents had arrived within a couple of days of each other and the other residents, well to say they lived in a world of their own was an understatement. Billy had learnt that Alzheimer's or dementia or whatever they wanted to call it, was known as the long goodbye and now he understood exactly what was meant. Sometimes Green Lawns seemed a lonely place for the residents as only George and Granny Davis received visitors and Billy was grateful for that. It might have sounded cruel but the others didn't know what day of the week it was let alone if anyone had come to see them. When Georges son and Granny Davis's granddaughter came to visit there were always tears. Neither recognised their family members and when George's son kept repeating Dad it's me your son the pleading in his voice was heartbreaking. It was during one of these visits that Billy tried to keep out of the way and decided to tidy up some of the rooms. Dulcie's was the first on the list and walking in he saw she was sitting in her chair and staring out of the window. Billy didn't speak to her and it wasn't because he couldn't be bothered. Many times he'd tried to make conversation with the people he cared for but there was never any kind of response, not unless you counted Edna trying to throw faeces at him or Ruby nipping him whenever he got in range of her hand. It was useless trying to get them to have a conversation; they just looked through him as if he were invisible. Picking up Dulcie's clothes from the floor, he folded them and was about to place them in the drawer when she spoke.

"About time some fucker tidied up in here, it's like a bleeding pigsty."

For a moment Billy was dumbstruck but after a second he placed the clothes onto the bed and walked over to her.

"Did you just speak to me?"

"Speak to you? of course I bleeding did, aint porky are you?"

Billy clapped his hands together as he laughed.

"So you aint do dally then?"

Dulcie Grey narrowed her eyes and frowned as she looked at him.

"Fucking do dally! You cheeky little sod of course I bleeding aint."

Billy sat down on the footstool in front of Dulcie's chair and studied her for a second. He'd been told that the residents could have the odd lucid moment but so far he hadn't been witness to any. He was a little confused and thought maybe it was one of those occasions.

"Well! What you looking at?"

"I'm not sure really. Either you're a very good

actress or you're having a few minutes where you actually know what's going on in the world?"
Dulcie leaned forward and swiped Billy gently across the top of the head but there was no real malice in her gesture.

"Hey!"

"Then don't be so bloody rude, I can't abide cheeky bleeding youngsters."

"So you really are normal then?"

"Normal!"

"Sorry but you know what I mean. You aint really like the others?"

"No I'm not but that's between you and me Billy boy, do you hear?"

Billy thought for a moment before he spoke. He knew he should tell Wendy about this but then again Dulcie must have her reasons for pretending she was like the others. Anyway he knew that if he did tell, then she would only act it out and make him look a fool.

"Ok it's our little secret but why would you want to be in a place like this if you aint lost your marbles?"

"Never you mind Billy boy, never you mind. Now if you'd be so good as to tidy this place up and then go. I'd be grateful for some privacy if you don't mind."

Billy did as he was asked and as he walked out of the door he turned and caught the smallest glimpse of a smile on Dulcie Grays face.

For the rest of the morning he couldn't get the old

woman out of his thoughts and by dinner break he was near to bursting. Deciding to do a little digging on the quiet he went outside to find Wendy. The small garden area was off limits to the residents and he knew Wendy Saxby could always be found under the metal fire escape having a crafty cigarette.
"Hi Billy what brings you out here?"
"Nothing really just thought I'd get a bit of fresh air. With the heating full on it gets a bit stifling in there sometimes."
"Tell me about it."
Wendy?"
"Yes Billy?
"What can you tell me about Dulcie Gray?"
Wendy suddenly became suspicious. For all her ranting and raving she loved the old people dearly and was overly protective of them, especially when someone started asking questions.
"Why do you want to know?"
Billy shrugged his shoulders.
"No reason really, it's just that all the others are like an open book and Dulcie isn't. I've never even heard her speak and I was just curious that's all."
"Hardly ever speaks to anyone does our Dulcie. She came here almost five years ago of her own free will."
"So she aint got dementia then?"
"Of course she has! You've only got to look at her to know that. As far as I'm aware she doesn't have any family, well none that have ever bothered to visit

her anyway. I do know she originally came from over Stepney way but that's about it really."
"So nothing exciting then, just another poor old sod left to fend for herself?"
"Yeah I suppose you could put it like that."
Wendy Saxby was just about to take the final drag of her cigarette when she felt liquid splash onto her head.
"What the fuck!!!"
Looking up through the metal slats she could see someone standing above her.
"Why you dirty old bitch!"
Billy followed her gaze and couldn't help but burst out laughing when he saw what was happening. Someone had left the fire escape door ajar and there stood Edna O'Brien, as naked as the day she was born and peeing directly onto Wendy's head.
"I don't bloody believe it; she's only gone and pissed on me."
Tears filled his eyes and Billy Jacobs was laughing so much that his sides were beginning to hurt.
"It aint bleeding funny mate, I'm going to have to wash me fucking hair now."
With that Wendy stormed inside and when Billy looked up again Edna had disappeared. She may have had dementia but at times Edna O'Brien knew exactly what she was doing.
Half an hour before his shift ended Billy decided to call in once more and see if Dulcie really was, for want of a better word normal.

Opening the door to her room he was about to use the ruse of checking on her towels but he didn't have to.

"Oh it's you again."

"Hello Dulcie I was just going to....."

Dulcie instantly cut him off.

"Going to, my arse! You've come in here to see if I'm away with the fairies again aint you?"

Billy smiled, she really was a wise old bird and putting her sharp manner to one side he was starting to warm to her.

"Got me bang to rights there me lady."

"Me Lady! You cheeky little sod? Well I aint so you can just bugger off young man and leave me in peace."

Billy Jacobs ignored Dulcie's order and instead once more took a seat on the footstool beside her.

"Dulcie?"

The woman didn't reply and continued to stare out of the window.

"Dulcie?"

At last she turned to look at him and after studying his face for a few seconds, she spoke.

"You still here?"

"I only want to talk to you Dulcie."

"Talk all you like Sonny but I aint got to answer you."

"Then why did you bother letting me know you can speak in the first place?"

"I'm just having a bit of fun I suppose, anything to

pass the time away and it aint as if you can tell anyone because they wouldn't believe you."
Dulcie began to chuckle. The sound of her laughter infuriated Billy and he now felt that she was mocking him. To begin with it had all been intriguing but now he felt a fool and that Dulcie Gray had just been playing with him.
"Please yourself but I aint going to waste my time trying to talk to someone who aint interested."
With that Billy walked from the room and after collecting his things, made his way home.
The next couple of days were hectic and it would be Friday before he had any real contact with Dulcie again. The early shift had begun as normal but when Billy went into Edna's room the poor old lady was almost gagging. Someone on the landing could be heard making the same noise and when he popped his head outside, Billy saw that it was Ruby Fulcher.
"Whatever's the matter love?"
Lawrence appeared from Dulcie's room and began to laugh.
"Don't worry son Ill sort it out. Vanna the new recruit has given them all the wrong teeth again. Same thing happened yesterday; they all resembled little snapping turtles at breakfast. I keep trying to explain that it aint a case of one size fits all but she don't speak much English. She nods her head but I know she aint got a bleeding clue what I'm on about."

After the breakfast things had been cleared away Wendy handed Billy a pile of neatly pressed linen and told him to take them to Edna and Dulcie's rooms. Doing as he was asked he quickly nipped in and out of Edna's before he could receive a nip or a bite. When he got to Dulcie Grays room he placed the items on the bed and opened her chest of drawers. About to put the items inside, he was momentarily stopped when she spoke to him again.
"Morning."
Billy wasn't angry anymore but he wasn't falling into the same trap he had a few days ago, so he ignored her and carried on with the linen.
"I said morning cloth ears!"
Still Billy didn't reply and he could now sense the tension in the air as Dulcie started to get agitated.
"Well I never! how bleeding rude. Your mother drag you up did she?"
That was the final straw and Billy marched over to the chair to confront her.
"Look old woman! Either speak to me or don't, I couldn't care less either way but don't play fucking games alright!"
Suddenly Dulcie began to chuckle and as much as it pained him to do so, Billy couldn't help but join in with her. Dulcie pointed to the footstool with her toe.
"Sit down Son."
After Billy was seated the two just stared at one another but it was Dulcie who was first to break the

silence.

"I was just testing you. I wanted to see if you had any backbone Billy and I think you have, even if you are a little slow."

"Hey!"

"What happened outside the other day, only I heard Saxby ranting about something. Old Edna flew down the fucking hall like the wind with Saxby chasing after her."

Billy told his new friend all about the peeing incident and Dulcie started to laugh so hard, that Billy was worried she might have a heart attack. Five minutes later and after he had handed Dulcie numerous tissues to wipe her eyes, she spoke again.

"So Billy boy, tell me about yourself."

"What do you want to know?"

"Everything. Let's start with where you live?"

"Hackney, on Ellingfort Road actually."

"With your Mum and Dad? And have you got a girlfriend or are you one of them fucking poofter's?"

"Bugger me Dulcie you don't half want to know a lot and anyway why should I reveal all when you won't tell me why you're here?"

"Maybe I will one day Billy boy but for now just indulge an old woman and tell me about yourself."

Billy smiled and began to reveal all about his life to the strange woman who liked to act mad but in reality was as sane as the next person, whatever that meant. He told her all about his early life and about having no father. In fact Billy went into every single detail even down to Sameer's shop and getting his collar felt with Johnny and Specs. Their conversation lasted for over an hour and occasionally Dulcie would interrupt him to ask the odd question but for the most part Billy just rambled on and revealed his whole life story to date.

"And there you have it, Billy Jacobs sad little life!"

"It aint sad love; I think you've had a lucky escape and now you're on the right track even if it did take you a while. Personally I aint ever had any time for coppers but I think that Harry Stanton did you a favour."

"There's no doubt about that Dulcie. I think, in fact I know, if it weren't for him I'd have become one of those drug addicts who mug little old ladies, just like you."

"I'd like to see you bleeding try Sonny. I might look knackered but there's still a lot of fight left in the old girl. Anyway, tell me a bit more about your Sally." Billy stood up and smoothed down his tunic. Glancing at his watch he was about to make his excuses but stopped dead in his tracks when he heard a strange voice.

Right! First number out tonight, we have two fat ladies eighty eight. L L L L lard arse. On its own, Kelly's eye number one. Clickety click sixty six tit wank. Oh fffffuck it, sorry! On the blue its......"

"Whoever's that?"

Dulcie began to laugh at the look of shock on Billy's

face.

"That my dear boy is Mac Long the bingo caller. He drops in every few months to give us a game or two. A right fucking shambles and no mistake. The poor bastards got tourettes but he don't charge them to do the calling so they overlook the language. Aint as if any of the poor fuckers in here would notice anyway!"

Billy stood rooted to the spot and laughed until he had tears in his eyes. It took a good few minutes and several deep breaths before he could compose himself.

"This place never stops amazing me Dulcie."
"You and me both Son!"
"Dulcie I'd love to stay and chat but if I don't get some work done, then Wendy's going to have my guts for garters. I'm off for the weekend but Ill pop in on Monday and we can have another talk. Oh and by the way it'll be your turn to reveal all."

With that Billy Jacobs leant down and tenderly kissed the top of Dulcie Grays head before walking from the room.

CHAPTER SEVEN

As promised Billy called in to see Dulcie Gray on Monday. It was just after lunch when most of the residents were taking a nap and things had quietened down. Glancing round to make sure that no one was within ear shot he knocked on the door and waited to be invited in. Dulcie couldn't risk being heard by anyone else and so ignored Billy's tap. After a few seconds he turned the handle and popped his head round the door.

"About bloody time."

"High there Dulcie how you doing?"

"Pissed off as usual but then what can I expect at my age. I'm full of bleeding aches and pains, it's like being a prisoner in this place."

Billy walked over to her chair and after giving her the widest smile he could muster, took his seat on the footstool in front of her.

"Now that's not true Dulcie and you know it. Why just this morning I saw you come back here with Lawrence."

"Well pardon me sonny! One bleeding trip out a week and I'm supposed to be grateful?"

"I can see you're in a bad mood sweetheart so maybe it aint the best time for a chat."

About to stand, Billy was stopped as her hand swiftly shot out and pressed down on his shoulder.

"I'm sorry, don't go Billy. Now tell me what you got up to this weekend."

Billy Jacobs removed the woman's hand from his shoulder but he didn't let go of it. As he continued to talk he tenderly held onto Dulcie Grays hand and he could tell that she found the gesture comforting.
"Now I told you last time I was here, the next conversation we would have was going to be about you."
"Get away with you. A young lad like you, don't want to be hearing about a beat up old woman's life."
"Yes I do. How about we make a deal. For every question you ask me, I get to ask you one back? It's called prit pro quo, I heard it in a film once."
Dulcie thought for a moment and then smiled.
"If I have to, but nothing too personal like and its quid pro quo not prit you little wanker."
Billy Jacobs laughed out loud.
"Oh listen to the bleeding encyclopaedia and no Dulcie, nothing too personal I promise."
Dulcie wriggled in her arm chair until she was fully upright. Things could get interesting and she was looking forward to it.
"Right then, as I asked before, what did you do at the weekend?"
"Not a lot really. Saturday I took Sally shopping, then out for a meal at night."
"Did you give her one?"
"Pardon?"
"Fuck me boy sometimes you seem so bleeding thick it beggars belief."

"I aint thick Dulcie but if you think I'm going to answer a question like that you can think again. Anyway why would you ask such a thing?"

"Look Sonny Jim, I may be ancient and not had me leg over in years but I still like to hear about it."

"Well you'll just have to use your imagination I'm afraid. Right my turn next, where do you go to every week with Lawrence?"

Dulcie Gray stared straight ahead and ignored his question.

"Dulcie?"

"You didn't answer my question so you aint playing the game."

Billy sighed loudly and proceeded to look at his watch. He would be leaving soon and he had hoped for a quick chat and then go home for a few hours relax. With Dulcie being awkward he somehow didn't think that was going to be the case now.

"Sometimes Dulcie you really are impossible. Alright! yes I got me leg over, happy now?"

"Where'd you do it."

"I aint answering any more questions about me sex life. Now shall we continue and it's your turn."

"He takes me to collect me pension and do a bit of shopping that's all. Now tell me about you and Sally, do you love her?"

Billy Jacobs was about to answer when the door suddenly flew open and Wendy Saxby's flushed face appeared round the door.

"Billy I know you're nearly off duty but Edna's just thrown a wobbly and attacked Ruby. Lawrence has got the afternoon off and I'm struggling my love. Any chance of a hand?"
Billy glanced at Dulcie and could tell by her expression that she wanted to give Wendy a right mouthful for interrupting. The only thing was, Dulcie hardly spoke to anyone, so she just had to stay silent and hold her anger inside. He wanted to laugh at the old woman's predicament. In the short time he had known Dulcie, Billy had quickly found out that keeping silent wasn't one of her best attributes and not being able to mouth off at Wendy must have been eating Dulcie up inside.
"I'll be back as soon as I can darling alright?"
With that he was gone and Dulcie was left to stew for what turned out to be two hours.
"Right I'm back, sorry about that."
"Fucking cheeky cow that Wendy, takes bleeding liberties she does."
"No she doesn't Dulcie, and if you would speak to people instead of letting them think you're ga ga then you'd be able to say something wouldn't you?"
"I'm alright as I am thank you very much. Anyway she's a nosey cow and if she thought I had all me faculties she'd be in here every bleeding five minutes. I don't think so, thank you very much. Now you was telling me about your Sally, do you love her?"
As Billy began to speak he was stopped for a second

when Dulcie took hold of his hand but he didn't comment on her action.

"Yes Dulcie, I do love her very much. Were trying to get a place of our own. Me Mums good but it would be nice to get some time alone. What with me working now, well that's proving a bit difficult. We went and looked at a couple of flats but they were the pits and my Sal's very particular.

"And so she should be. Now then Billy boy old Dulcie here might just be able to help you out."

"If you're going to offer me money then thanks but no. Firstly I aint allowed to take anything from the residents and secondly I've got me pride you know and ...."

Dulcie Gray squeezed his hand as tightly as she could manage but due to her age it felt more like a gentle stroke to Billy.

"I wasn't about to offer you me life savings dozy bollocks. Now just listen will you. I've got a little house though no one else is privy to that fact and that's the way I want it to stay. The place is standing empty so if you wanted to rent it then you'd be doing me a favour."

Momentarily stunned, Billy was speechless. This sounded too good to be true and deep down he knew that it would probably turn out to be nothing.

"How come you've got a house if you're in here?"

"because no one knows. The government are greedy bastards and if they knew about it they'd sell it off to pay for this place."

"So why don't you live there? Why on earth would you want to be here when you've got your own place?"

For a moment Dulcie didn't reply and as Billy studied her face he could see the onset of tears begin. It was only a second before her hand swiftly wiped them away and she sniffed loudly.

"Loneliness I suppose, now do you want it because I won't bleeding offer again?"

Billy Jacobs didn't know what to say. If he said no, then that was it. On the other hand it could be in some remote place and in a rundown state.

Billy stood up and stared out of the window. He didn't want to hurt her feelings but at the same time he had to be truthful. Deciding that he'd let her down gently he spoke.

"Can I, we, have a look at it first."

"Alright but not a word to anyone. Fetch me bag over and I'll get you the keys. Now it's on a small road at the back of Liverpool street station, Bell Lane alright? The numbers on the key ring"

Billy couldn't believe his ears. Properties in that part of London sometimes went for millions of pounds and he started to wonder if Dulcie was really nuts after all.

"Sweetheart are you really sure about this?"

Dulcie Grey looked up from her chair and frowned. "Look you're a nice boy and you don't seem to mind giving up your time for me so I'd like to return the favour. Now take as long as you like and let me

know what you think next week."
Billy graciously took the keys and after kissing her on the cheek, left the room to begin the walk home. The rest of the week passed quickly. With double shifts and late duty it was Sunday before he had a chance to view the place. Originally he was going to go alone, as he didn't want to build Sally's hopes up but after having second thoughts he'd decided to take a chance and surprise her, after all nothing ventured nothing gained.
It was just after ten when Sally rang the bell and as Jackie had been hitting the vodka heavier than usual the previous night, it was Billy who answered the door.
"Hi Babe! So where you taking me today?"
"It's a surprise."
Sally Durrant grinned, she liked surprises and since Billy had got his job it had been one surprise after another. He was always taking her out to dinner and buying her little presents.
Making their way up west, the couple entered Petticoat Lane and shopped till they dropped. Billy brought them both matching T-shirts and after stopping off for hot bagels at Kossoff's Jewish bakery, Sally assumed they would make their way home. Instead of heading towards the tube Billy lead Sally onto Goulston Street before turning left into Bell lane. The road was a lot bigger than Billy imagined, after hearing the word Lane he was expecting something small and when he stopped

outside the house he couldn't believe his eyes. From the ground the house was three storeys high and had two large roman style columns at either side of the front door. The red paintwork was peeling but all in all the place didn't look in such a bad state. Walking up the steps he stopped when he realised that Sally wasn't with him. Turning back, he could only smile when he saw the look of bewilderment on her face.

"Look babe, just humour me will you. Let's get inside and I'll explain everything alright?"

Sally Durrant didn't say a word but she was so curious that she did as her boyfriend asked. Placing the key that Dulcie had given him into the lock, Billy turned the handle. Five years worth of junk mail had accumulated behind the door and he had to push hard to get it open. The smell inside was musty but nothing too bad and as he walked from room to room he almost forgot that Sally was with him. Reaching the large back kitchen he began to shake his head and with the realisation of just what was on offer, he began to laugh.

"Right Billy Jacobs that's it. Either you tell me what the hell is going on or I'm out of here."

Billy walked over to where she stood and taking her in his arms he embraced her for several seconds.

"I think I've met me fairy godmother Sal."

"Have you been at the wacky backy Billy?"

Guiding her to the bottom of the staircase Billy Jacobs sat down and began to tell her all about

Dulcie Gray and the incredible offer she'd made him."

"So how much is it going to cost us a month?"

" I don't know yet we aint talked money but I'm sure it won't be a massive amount, after all Dulcie knows I don't earn a mint."

"And what about when the old girl pops her clogs?"

"Sal!"

"Well is there going to be some distant relative turn up and put us out on the street?"

"Fuck me! Why do you have to be so negative all the time. As far as I know Dulcie aint got any family. Now don't look a gift horse in the mouth. Can we just enjoy the moment and perhaps get a little excited?"

Silently Sally mouthed the word sorry and then blew him a kiss.

Within seconds Sally Durrant was running from room to room and shrieking with happiness.

By the time they had finished exploring they had counted five bedrooms, four on the first floor and one very large room right at the top of the house. There was only one bathroom but laughing, Sally said she could live with that. On the ground floor there were two large reception rooms and a kitchen not to mention a basement. Billy had tried the door under the stairs that led down to the basement but he just shrugged his shoulders when he found it was locked.

"I know it needs a bit of work, some decorating here

and there but well all in all it aint too bad. That's about it, so what do you think then?"

Sally flung her arms around Billy's neck and lifting her legs from the ground, wrapped them tightly around his waist.

"I think it's wonderful!"

Later that afternoon as the couple finally made their way home they chatted nonstop about the house and how lucky they were.

Before they entered his mothers flat Sally stopped and grabbing hold of Billy's arms turned him to face her.

"Now Billy when you've sorted out the finances I think I need to meet this Dulcie Gray and we need to find out a bit more about her."

Billy Jacobs rolled his eyes upwards but he didn't let Sally see him. Dulcie was a rare breed of woman, the kind that you didn't come across very often and he didn't know just what Sally would make of her. Never the less Billy agreed that later the following week he would take Sally to Green lawns and introduce the two. It wasn't something he was looking forward to so for the time being he tried to put it to the back of his mind and just enjoy this happy time.

CHAPTER EIGHT

On Monday morning Billy began the early shift. As he walked through the door the clock in the hall struck seven. He was desperate to talk to Dulcie but things at Green Lawns were manic to say the least. Lawrence was off sick and as yet the agency staff hadn't turned up, so it was all hands on deck. After helping Wendy to dress Ruby, the pair now had it down to a fine art, Billy moved on to Edna. As usual she was covered in faeces and his first job was to shower her. It took over half an hour as Edna was in a bad mood and wouldn't cooperate. Finally after much coaxing the task was complete and the residents were now all seated at the breakfast table. After spooning a small amount of cereal into Granny's mouth Billy looked in Dulcie's direction but she didn't acknowledge him. He'd been so excited about the house and now he was worried that she might have changed her mind.
By eleven things had calmed down enough for him to take a break and he made his way up to Dulcie Grays room. As usual she was seated in her chair but she didn't immediately speak when he walked in. For a few moments he stood beside her dreading starting up a conversation for fear of what she might say but finally he plucked up the courage.
"So, how's things with you today?"
"Bleeding stupid question that is. How do you

think they are?"

Walking towards the door Billy had decided that she wasn't in a good mood and rather than hear her retract her offer he would give her a while to cheer up.

"And where do you think you're going young man?"

Billy smiled, for some reason Dulcie like to play silly games. He didn't have a clue why she was like she was but he knew he had to play along with her.

"I didn't think you was in the mood to talk."

"Did I say that?"

"No you didn't."

"Then come over here and tell me what you thought of it."

For the next fifteen minutes Billy Jacobs relayed all that had happened the previous day. He told of Sally's excitement but also of her worries.

"So you see Dulcie, we love the house, we would love to live there but there are a few loose ends that need tying up."

Dulcie thought for a minute. She really liked Billy, no it was deeper than that she was really fond of him. Dulcie was glad that he was questioning her but how much she should tell him was another matter.

"Billy boy I'm going to put your mind at rest but there are a few things I can't tell you. Now don't ask me why because you won't get an answer. As for the rent, I thought about fifty a week, how's that sound?"

"It sounds too good to be true."

"Don't look a gift horse in the mouth lad. That's what I want and not a penny more. I didn't offer you the place to make money out of you; I just wanted to help you both. As for me popping me clogs. Well as long as you pay the bills then you can live there as long as you want."

"But how is......"

"Look I've already said there's things I aint going to tell you, now leave it at that. How would you like it if someone kept trying to pry into your private business? Right you can move in when you like and you can do what you want to the place as long as you don't fucking knock it down."

"I don't know what to say."

"You aint got to say anything, now I'm a bit tired so if you don't mind I'd like to have a nap."

Billy smiled and walked towards the door but stopped when he remembered what Sally had said.

"Just one more thing Dulcie."

"Now what?"

"It's nothing really, only Sal said she would like to meet you."

"Sorry Billy but if you start bringing people here to see me then old Saxby's going to wonder why. Tell your young lady that under other circumstances I would love to make her acquaintance but for now it just aint possible."

"I understand and Dulcie."

"For fucks sake now what?"
"Thanks."
The next few weeks were busy beyond belief. Billy was still doing double shifts and any spare time was spent at the house. Walls were stripped of the original paper and every surface was cleaned from top to bottom. When Billy finished work late he would make his way over to Bell Lane to make sure Sally got home safely. Every afternoon when she'd finished college she would go to the house and get as much done as possible. Billy was amazed at how hard Sally worked and his heart swelled with love, even when she was covered in dust and had scraps of wall paper stuck in her hair. The couple hadn't shown Jackie the house yet and were a little concerned how they would explain things when they eventually did take her to see it. Dulcie Gray insisted on a daily update and Billy was happy to oblige. The woman seemed pleased with everything they were doing but when he told her they had painted the bedroom black she screwed up her face.

"Fucking black! Your having a laugh aint you? Aint in some kind of cult are you?"
"It's the fashion Dulcie."
"Bleeding fashion you must be mad. Still it's your place now so do what you like."
"When it's finished I'd like you to come and see it, maybe have a spot of tea with us."
"No!!!!!!"

Dulcie Gray's words had come out in a scream and it unnerved Billy. Kneeling down beside her he took both of Dulcie's hands in his.

"Sweetheart! Whatever's the matter?"

"I aint going back there and you can't make me."

"Of course I can't and I wouldn't want to."

"Then leave it at that will you. Now piss off Billy and I don't want to hear another word about that fucking place alright?"

To say he was confused was an understatement, one minute the old gal had wanted a blow by blow account now she seemed almost petrified at the mention of the place. It was obvious that something had really upset Dulcie but just what that was he didn't have a clue. Billy Jacobs had grown to love the old lady and not just because she'd helped him out. The last thing he wanted to do was hurt her so from now on any mention of the house on Bell Lane was a taboo subject. The couple still had their daily chats but they steered cleared of anything to do with DIY or houses.

As Lawrence was now back at work Billy had the whole weekend off and after getting up early on Saturday morning, he made his way over to the house. Sally said she would join him at lunch time and as he let himself in Billy couldn't help but smile. The place was now painted in warm cream tones and it had a homely welcoming feel. After putting the kettle on Billy noticed a long list of jobs to be done, which Sally had neatly written out and pinned to the back of the door. With the two upper floors finished the couple were now concentrating on the main sitting room. Billy selected his paint brushes and then waited for the kettle to boil. As he leaned up against the sink unit and drank his tea he glanced in the direction of the hall and spied the basement door. In all the time that he'd been coming here he'd been too busy to deal with the locked door and now curiosity was starting to get the better of him. Placing his cup on the drainer, he made his way over and pulled at the door handle. It wouldn't budge but that just made Billy more determined. Looking round the kitchen he found a large flat headed screwdriver and began to lever it between the locked door and frame. He didn't want to damage anything but then again he was quite capable of putting on a new lock should the need arise. As Billy began to prise the door open he thought back to Dulcie getting upset when he mentioned bringing her here. Suddenly and for some reason, he didn't know why but going into the basement scared him but he was also intrigued. He knew he should just leave things as they were and keep his nose out but something deep inside wouldn't let him. Billy's hands began to shake and he threw the screwdriver to the floor and went back into the kitchen. Now a little calmer he once again boiled the kettle and made more tea. At this rate he would still be in the kitchen when Sally arrived and then there would be hell to pay when she saw that

he'd hardly got any work done. With a cup in one hand and a paintbrush in the other he made his way to the sitting room and began to paint. As hard as he tried he couldn't concentrate as his thoughts kept going back to the basement door. Billy didn't know why it was playing so heavily on his mind; it wasn't as if they needed more space. As things were he didn't have a clue how they were going to furnish the house so why worry about rooms in the basement that they didn't even need.
"Oh fuck it!"
Billy looked down to see that he'd spilt the entire pot of gloss paint onto the wooden floor, the floor that it had taken him days to sand down. Sighing heavily he went to find a rag to mop up the mess but as he once more passed the basement door he knew that no matter what, he had to go down there. It was hard enough spending his spare time here but once they actually moved in it would be impossible not to find out what was lurking below and why the door had been locked. For a moment he imagined himself in some Hitchcock movie and the thought made him laugh and speak out loud.
"Billy Jacobs you really are a twat sometimes!" Fuck me if Sal could hear me talking to myself she'd think I've gone as fucking loopy as the old gals I look after."
He spent ages clearing up the spilled paint but the locked basement door was still nagging away in his brain and when it wouldn't go away he decided to

take action. Entering the hall he stooped down to pick up the screwdriver and then marched over to the door and set to work on the offending wood like a man possessed. Finally he heard the lock snap and stood back to admire his handy work. After getting his mind in gear, breaking open the door had been relatively easy and there wasn't much sign of any real damage done. Cautiously he peered inside. Billy had watched enough programmes on the telly to know that some old places often had rotten staircases. When everything looked alright he flicked on the old round light socket and ventured down the stairs. The air smelled musty and more than a little damp, something Billy made a mental note to look into. Particles of dust hung in the rays from the over head light and as they filled his nostrils it made Billy feel like coughing. The basement should have covered the entire area of the house but it looked so small and as far as he could make out only contained the one room. It was littered with piles of old newspapers and bending down to inspect one, he noticed that the date was nineteen forty five. Billy jumped when he heard a sound and thought it might be rats but chastised himself when he realised that it was only the door above that had closed. Rummaging around he didn't find much of interest and was about to go back upstairs, when he spied another door at the rear of the room which was partially hidden by a stack of old tea chests. This looked interesting and glancing at his watch he knew that he had a couple of hours before Sally arrived. She would do her nut that he hadn't got much work done but he could soon get her onside and besides this was proving to be much more fun than painting the skirting's. One by one Billy moved the crates out of the way and trying the handle he expected it to be locked. It wasn't and as the door creaked open he peered in. The room was slightly smaller than the first and was stacked from floor to ceiling with old furniture. There were no priceless antiques but it was still all good stuff, the kind of things you would see in an old wartime film. Billy knew that Sally wouldn't want any of it but then if it helped fill the upper rooms, for the time being at least, it would help. After opening a few drawers and finding nothing of interest he spotted a large brass standard lamp. The shade was a bit dated but if he put on a modern one it could pass muster and might look alright in one of the bedrooms. Picking it up he inspected the tall metal shaft and seeing no damage he decided to take it back upstairs. As he swung round sideways with the lamp in his hands the base crashed into a wall and Billy stopped immediately. He wasn't concerned with damaging anything, what bothered him was the hollow sound that he'd heard as the lamp made contact with the old wall. Walking over he studied the area and noticed that the plaster work was crazed and a different colour to the other walls. Rubbing his hand over the surface a piece of

loose plaster fell away. Billy poked at one of the joints with his finger and a brick fell inwards disappearing into an unknown space. Billy Jacobs pushed even harder on several more bricks and they too disappeared.
"What the fuck!"
Suddenly from upstairs he heard voices and knew for the time being that he would have to abandon his investigation.
"Billy! Billy love where are you?"
Sally was early and now she would give him a right ear bashing, still there was nothing he could do about that now.
"Coming babe."
Billy could hear footsteps moving about in the kitchen above and he knew he had to get back up there before she tried to venture down into the basement.
"I've brought your Mum to see the place!"
This was all he needed. With Jackie nosing about he wouldn't get a chance to delve any further till tomorrow. Climbing the stairs he switched off the light and closed the door. Billy looked flustered as he tried to brush the lime dust from his clothes.
"What on earth were you doing down there?"
"Nothing. Hi Mum you alright?"
Jackie Lemon couldn't believe what she was seeing. Her Son had a place of his own and what a place it was. She kissed Billy on the cheek and tenderly touched the side of his face.

"I'm right proud of you Son and no mistake. Now are you going to show your old Mum what you've been doing?"

"Yeah you show Jackie round and I'll go have a look in the basement."

As Sally placed her hand on the door handle and pushed Billy grabbed her by the arm and he used a little more force than was necessary.

"Billy! That hurt, don't be so rough."

"Sorry babe but I don't want you going down there, the stairs aint safe. Probably why the door was kept locked."

Sally thought no more of it and as she lead Jackie upstairs busily chatted away about wallpaper and colour charts.

Billy Jacobs pulled the door shut and leaning back against the wall exhaled deeply. He didn't know why he'd over reacted, it wasn't as if he'd found anything untoward but deep inside he had a bad feeling about what secrets the basement held.

CHAPTER NINE

Saturday night had been spent at the flat on Ellingfort Road with Jackie. So happy about the house news she'd made a lovely celebratory meal but Billy wasn't up for conversation. Sally had tried and tried but his replies were short and none too sweet. After watching half of Heartbeat, which bored her to tears with its constant sixties music, she was slowly getting angrier and angrier. Suddenly Sally stood up and grabbed her coat from the arm of the chair.
"Well if you're going to stay in such a shitty mood all night I might as well go."
Jackie Lemon was so engrossed in her programme that she didn't take any notice when Sally stormed out into the hall. Billy, realising that he'd overstepped the mark, was up like a shot. Grabbing her arm he managed to stop her just as she was about to walk through the door.
"Don't go Sal, I'm sorry."
"Whatever's wrong with you tonight?"
"I don't know I'm probably over tired that's all.
Sally Durrant studied his face and he did look worn out. With all the excitement of the house she hadn't really given much thought to the amount of hours he'd been putting in.
"I'm sorry babe; you do look a bit tired. I tell you what, why don't you take tomorrow off from the house and catch up with your sleep. I've got a ton

of course work to get through so it'll do us both good to have a rest."

Her words were like music to his ears and Billy kissed her passionately.

"Hold on a minute mate. If you think me suggesting you take some time off is an excuse to get into me knickers, you can think again."

"I wasn't thinking any such thing and besides I'm too tired to get a lob on. Me old boy thinks he's gone into retirement."

Sally laughed out loud and her cheeks flushed at his words.

"Shush or your mum will hear. Now are you going to walk me home or what?"

Billy wasn't happy about lying to her but still, he was relieved that tomorrow he would be able to get on with his investigations undisturbed.

Jackie Lemon allowed herself the luxury of a lay in every Sunday morning and today was no exception. Finally getting up at around ten she saw her son's bedroom door was still closed and decided to let him sleep in. The poor kid really was working hard and as much as she'd prayed for him to get a job, with the double shifts and doing up the house, Jackie worried that it was all a bit too much. In reality Billy had been gone for hours. He'd set his alarm for six and after dressing and leaving the flat as quietly as he could, had set off for Bell Lane. The market was just setting up in Middlesex Street. In a couple of hours time it would be packed with tourists, all desperate to visit the historical Petticoat lane, unaware that there hadn't been anywhere with that name for over a hundred and fifty years. The prudish Victorians had changed it as they didn't think it correct to refer to under garments but no one had bothered to inform the tourists of that fact. As they laid out their wares stall holders shouted out to one another and no one gave Billy a second glance. Not that it would have mattered but for some reason Billy felt uneasy as if a thousand pairs of eyes were watching him.

When the house came into sight Billy felt a shiver run down his spine. He knew he was being ridiculous but he couldn't help himself. Taking a deep breath he climbed the steps and made his way inside. The place was deathly quiet and he could feel his heart pounding in his chest. He tried to pull himself together. This was going to be his home and he wanted to feel happy when he stepped over the threshold. Billy Jacobs wasn't stupid; he knew that he had no evidence of anything untoward down in the basement. All he'd found was a few loose bricks in a wall but no matter how hard he tried to convince himself, a nagging feeling of foreboding just wouldn't go away. Billy was better prepared than he'd been yesterday. Today he'd brought a hammer, a torch, some old sacks and a spare light bulb. Walking into the kitchen he switched on the radio. Bucks Fizz burst into life singing 'Making your Mind up' and the house began to feel a bit cheerier. After switching on the basement light he slowly descended the staircase. Now familiar with the surroundings, he felt a little easier as he made his way through to the second room. Nothing had changed; the furniture was still stacked high and the lamp was lying on the floor where he'd dropped it. Suddenly Billy felt like an idiot and shook his head at what a complete fool he'd been. Still he was here now so he might as well take a closer look and in any case he needed to find out about the damp and just what was behind the wall in case it was dangerous. Expecting it to take some time he was surprised when after hitting the first brick, a large square about two foot wide fell inwards. Knocking out several more bricks so that he could squeeze through Billy shone his torch around the space. Dust and cobwebs hung in the air like a scene from some horror movie and a tingle ran down his spine. The room was about twenty feet square and only slightly larger than his mothers lounge back at the flat. When he noticed a ceiling rose he pushed in the bulb he'd brought and hoped for the best. After feeling round for a switch, his fingers at last struck lucky and he flicked it on. Amazingly it worked and the area was soon lit, albeit very dimly. Shadows fell heavily around the perimeter giving the space an eerie feel. Scanning the walls he couldn't see anything and was about to turn round when something in the corner caught his eye. He hadn't noticed it at first as it was hidden by the shadows but now Billy moved in for a closer look. The shape was narrow and about six feet long. To begin with Billy thought it was just the remnants of a piece of carpet that had long since rotted away. He prodded it with his foot and white dust flew about in all directions. Bending down he could now see that it wasn't carpet but something wrapped in the remains of an old army blanket. The acid taste of fear began to build in his mouth and as Billy pulled back a corner of the material a bony hand fell out. Billy screamed and fell backwards. Suddenly the overhead bulb popped and he was showered with fragments of glass. Panting heavily and with his heart pounding in his chest Billy fumbled on the ground for his torch. Finally he breathed a sigh of relief when his hand at last touched the cold steel. His breath made a panting sound as he inched forward for another look and could feel his whole body begin to tremble. Pulling back what was left of the blanket revealed a partial skeleton. He could just make out pieces of cloth that resembled some kind of uniform and Billy guessed it was Second World War. The flesh had long since disintegrated so there was no bad smell and Billy studied what was left of the corpse for several minutes. Finally he sat on the ground and propped his back up against the wall. He really had to think about this. If he did nothing, could he still live here? God! If Sal ever found out it would be the end of everything before they had

even moved in. On the other hand he knew it was his duty to go to the police but then that would open up a whole can of worms. There was Dulcie to consider and God above knew how involved she was in all of this. Even if she wasn't aware of it, he would still lose the house. Billy Jacobs was in turmoil and standing up he shone his torch around the rest of the outer walls.
"Oh no! Please God no!"
On the opposite wall to the first set of remains was a similar shape and as he inched closer Billy knew only too well what he was about to uncover. This too was only a partial corpse but after he'd poked at it with the end of his torch Billy could see that it was a woman. The remainder of her clothes were just like Billy had seen in old black and white movies. The poor soul was in the same state as the first with no skin and not very many bones. It was as if someone had attempted to apply some kind of accelerant to dispose of them quicker. Whoever it was hadn't done a very good job and the cold stare of a skeleton glared back at him. Poking at the remains caused lime dust to swirl up from the remaining fabric. Billy Jacobs sighed heavily but for some reason wasn't as shocked as he had been on examining the first body. Praying that there wasn't any more he scanned the other walls with his torch. Relief washed over him when nothing more came to light and deciding he needed to sit down began to make his way from the room. About to climb the

first stair tread he was stopped when a couple of loose slabs on the floor, began to rock under his feet. Bending down, Billy was only inspecting them to see if they would have to be re-laid but something forced him to look closer. Lifting a corner he hauled up the first slab and then quickly followed with the second. Staring at the soil he could make out the form of a heart that had been pressed neatly into the soil with little stones. Deciding that after what he'd just found he had to explore further, Billy picked up an old rusty trowel from the floor and began to dig away at the earth. Suddenly he fell backwards again as he realised what he was unearthing. Sweat stood out on his brow and his whole body shook as he gazed down at a third set of remains. Pulling himself together he gently continued the task but now his exploration was in a gentler manner. This body was much smaller and where the other two had been roughly concealed, with this one someone had taken their time. From the size Billy could see that it must be a child and that realisation alone made him want to cry. The skeleton was neatly wrapped in a floral eiderdown and unlike the other two; this one appeared to be complete. Lying on top of the corpse was a small book and after picking it up and brushing off the earth, Billy realised it was a little white bible. He didn't know what to do next and was in turmoil regarding leaving it as it was or covering it over again. Walking back up the stairs, Billy closed the door and made his way into the kitchen. He decided a cup of tea would calm him but as he plugged in the kettle he could visibly see his hands were still shaking and his shirt was wringing with perspiration. Two hours later and he was still sitting at the small table his mother had brought the couple. Finally he decided that he had no alternative but to visit Dulcie, that or he would go crazy thinking about it all. Locking the front door he was about to head in the direction of Green Lawns Manor but then thought better of it. If he turned up when he was supposed to have a day off it would only arouse suspicion, especially dressed as he was and covered in dust. No this would have to wait until tomorrow, though how he would ever get any sleep was beyond Billy Jacobs.

Just as he'd expected sleep evaded Billy for most of the night and Jackie had been forced to physically shake him awake the next morning to get a response. It was long after midnight before Billy managed to get some sleep and now just a few hours later he had to get up again.

"Come on son you're going to be late."

"What's the time?"

"Gone six thirty, the poor old buggers are going to be starving by the time you get to work."

Feeding Granny, Ruby and the rest of the clan was the furthest thing from Billy Jacobs mind but he flew out of bed all the same. After a quick wash and declining his mother's offer of breakfast, Billy was out of the door in less than fifteen minutes.

Running for most of the way he actually managed to make it to work on time, though he was red faced and panting as he rang the bell to be let in.
Desperate to confront Dulcie he'd actually gotten a foot on the first stair tread when he was stopped by Wendy Saxby.
"Hold on a minute Billy, I need you to take one of the residents out today. It can wait until after breakfast but Dulcie needs to collect her pension and Lawrence has called in sick again"
The news was music to Billy's ears and he made his way into the dining room to help with the others. After all the breakfast duties had been carried out and the plates cleared away he seized his opportunity. Billy found Dulcie seated in the hall, dressed in her best coat ready to go out.
The mini cab collected Dulcie Gray and Billy Jacobs at precisely ten o'clock. Not a word passed between them during the journey and when they reached Victoria Park Road Billy asked the driver to pull up outside Evans cafe.
"Oi! What the fuck are you doing this aint the Post Office?"
Billy turned to look at his companion and she could see that his face was ashen.
"No it aint Dulcie but if you know what's good for you then you won't complain. I don't want to hear another word until were inside and seated"
About to protest Dulcie thought better of it. She couldn't work out what was wrong with her friend

today. To begin with it had crossed her mind that it was something to do with the house but she dismissed that idea instantly. The driver eyed the two in his rear view mirror, he wasn't sure what was going on but he had no intention of getting involved. So long as the fare was paid by someone then he didn't give a monkeys what happened. Passing over a ten pound note that Wendy had given him, Billy slowly escorted Dulcie's from the cab. Holding her arm as they entered the cafe, Billy led her to a table that was situated in a quiet corner. After making sure she was seated properly he walked up to the counter to order two teas. Dulcie didn't mind being here, in fact it made a change but she was a bit miffed that he hadn't even asked her what she wanted. Billy sat down opposite the old lady and was about to launch into a speech he'd prepared earlier but he didn't get the chance.
"Well I thought that was a bit fucking rude, not asking me what I wanted."
Billy shook his head in amazement.
"Get used to it because where you're going to end up you won't get no choice in what you fucking have."
Dulcie started to get annoyed. She was fond of Billy, very fond indeed but she wasn't about to be talked to like that from anyone. Billy Jacobs could change his attitude this instant, or she was going to get up and leave right now.
"Whatever I've supposed to have done just fucking

tell me or old Dulcie here's going to walk."
"OK, you asked for it. There happens to be three fucking dead bodies in the basement of that house you've just rented to me. Now I aint sure what you know but I don't think it's the fucking norm, not unless it's the new fashion!"
"Oh! So you know then?"
"Fucking know!!!"
Billy's tone had become raised and Dulcie glanced in all directions hoping no one had heard him.
"Alright! Alright! calm down will you. I didn't think you'd go down there let alone go knocking down walls."
"It happened by accident and don't start making fucking excuses Dulcie, just tell me what's going on will you?"
Dulcie scratched her chin in a nonchalant manner as if she was deciding what shoes to buy and it irritated Billy to boiling point.
"We aint moving till you tell me! Well sit her all fucking day if that's what it takes."
Dulcie Gray could see he was serious and that now after all these years she was going to have to tell someone the truth about her life. She could feel a lump in her throat and her hands were clammy. Dulcie preferred Billy to think that she was strong and that there wasn't much that bothered her but in reality, nothing could be further from the truth.
"Ok but it's a long story and it aint very pretty."
"Pretty!!! What the fuck......."

"Don't start again, I'm going to tell you. It's just that it was a long time ago and I aint never breathed a word to another living soul. Now do you want the short version or the long one?"

Billy looked annoyed; he was desperate for her to get to the point.

"I know you think I'm dragging this out Billy boy but I need to explain everything before you judge me."

"I aint judging you."

"You will! Believe me by the time I get to the end of me story you will probably have me hung drawn and fucking quartered. Any way where was I? I think you need to hear it all so you can understand it properly. This is going to take some doing. See a lot of what happened was down to events that happened long before I lived in Bell Lane and it was told to me by someone else and oh well here goes. Hold onto your bleeding hat because it's going to be a bumpy ride. For me at least, it all began in nineteen forty when I was just thirteen. It was the beginning of the war and it weren't any fun I can tell you! Well that's about as far back as I can remember, though really it's a bit irrelevant but......"

"Dulcie!"

"Alright alright! I suppose I should really start at the very beginning and if what I was told is true, that would be back in nineteen twenty one, see in those times............"

CHAPTER TEN
1921

Today its known as Tower Hamlets in Stepney but when the Leicester's were residents no such place existed. Jamaica Street was a row of terraced houses; in fact the whole area was row upon row of terraced houses. After the slum clearances the area had been built to house the displaced poor and immigrants, who were not wanted in the affluent addresses of the capital.

Ethel Leicester had tried to raise her three boys to have decent moral values. It was the only way she had known but it hadn't been easy. Taking in washing and chopping kindling had provided enough to put food on the table but very little else. He husband had been off the scene since the birth of Joey ten years earlier. Life was one continual slog and when Ethel contracted consumption her death was swift. Albie the eldest Leicester child, had been forced to take over the parental role. At twenty years old and with two younger brothers it had been a difficult job but as the years passed life slowly began to form some sort of normality. Money for Albie had never been a problem; he'd always had his finger in numerous pies. What Albie had struggled with was raising his brothers. Not so much with Archie as they were so close in age but young Joey had been a different kettle of fish. The boy skipping school and having the old bill constantly knocking on the door was not good for Albie's line of business. Albie Leicester was and always would be the head of the family and Archie, though only two years younger than his brother did everything he was told. Eventually Joey would see his brothers more like Dads and show them the respect they craved and in return he was spoilt rotten.

Ten years later and the Leicester's were a force to be reckoned with. Forerunners to the likes of the Kray's and Foreman's the Leicester brothers saw themselves as modern day Robin Hoods. They gave to the poor and robbed from the rich, at least that's how they saw things. In reality they were bully's who indeed stole from the rich and sold on, at exorbitant prices, to the poor. Revered by all around them they took exactly what they wanted when they wanted. Local shopkeepers were afraid to ask for payment and none was ever offered. The family home was small and business was run from the front room. Their own little posse gave all the protection that was needed and for a long time things ran smoothly.

They were yet to be of any real interest to the police, so for now things were moving nicely along. Daily meetings would be held in the house on Jamaica Street and everyone was expected to attend. Joey, now twenty himself was the only one to be granted an exception. As far as he saw it, he was his own man and took little notice of his older brothers. A bully, he had throughout his teens instilled fear in all of the other kids in the area. It wasn't that he was hard or had any great fighting ability. It was simply that when Joey didn't get his own way he would threaten to get his brothers. It was a threat that all the other kids took seriously. Not for themselves but they were well aware that any kid who upset Joey Leicester would have revenge taken out on their parents.

The brothers had recently moved into the protection racket and the local pub owners were paying out big time. The payments were handed over begrudgingly and it was getting to the stage where some publicans were losing up to half of their weekly takings. Most of the public houses in the East End were now under the control of the Leicester's. The two most profitable were The Carpenters Arms in Bethnal Green which would eventually be bombed out in world war two and The White Hart situated on Whitechapel high street. Peter Rathbone had initially inherited the white Hart from his father. Intending to run the place for just a few weeks, he had instantly fallen in love with the trade but since the arrival of the Leicester's, business had dropped dramatically. Regulars had dwindled for fear of the brothers but the protection money was rising by the month. Peter Rathbone was almost at braking point and had decided to front out Archie Leicester when he came to collect one Friday night. It was early summer, the sun was shining and the front doors were wide open. Peter was getting ready for his one busy time of the week when Archie entered.

"Right then Petey boy! Time to pay your dues."
Peter Rathbone hated being called Petey but had always been too afraid to speak out. Well tonight was going to be different, tonight Peter would make a stand not only for himself but for every other Publican in the East End.

"Look Archie, I mean Mr Leicester I'm having a bit of a problem meeting me payment this week and I was wondering......"

Archie Leicester held up his palms and took a step forward, in fear Peter at the same time took a step backwards.

"That aint fucking good enough Petey boy. Now if I go back to me brother without your reddies he aint going to be a happy bunny and you really don't want to see Albie when he aint happy!"

"But Mr Leicester....."

Peter Rathbone didn't get a chance to finish his sentence before he went flying a cross one of the pub tables. His weight caused the table to collapse and Peter ended up in a heap on the floor. Instantly his jaw began to swell and he prayed it wasn't broken. Archie left the White Hart after informing Peter that he'd be back tomorrow and his money had better be waiting.

Reaching the house on Jamaica Street Archie

Leicester was reluctant to go inside. He knew Albie would blow his stack even though they had money coming in from all directions. To Albie it wasn't about the cash, it was about face and the fact that some tosser couldn't be seen to be getting one over on the family. Archie took a deep breath and entered the sitting room where for once it was only his two brothers in residence. Normally there was a houseful and Albie seemed to take pleasure in belittling his brother in front of other people.

"Right let's have a count up. How much did you bring in today Arch?"

"Bit light I'm afraid, that tosser over at the White Hart made all the excuses under the sun. I told him I'd go back tomorrow."

Albie Leicester was soon out of his armchair and standing so close to Archie that he could feel the heat of his brother's breath.

"Fucking told him you'd be back tomorrow? What are you some kind of soft cunt all of a sudden. Get back round there and tell that cunt its only because of my generous nature that he's still fucking breathing fresh air."

"Look Albie I hear what you're saying but the wanker aint got the cash so there's no point in going back today."

"I don't give a flying fuck if he's got the money or not. Smash the fucking place up, knock seven bells of shit out of him. Just let it be known that the Leicester's aint to be messed with. I want our name

alone, to be enough to instil fear into every cunt from here to lands fucking end. That way the tossers will think twice before ever grassing us."
Joey piped up and his enthusiasm pleased Albie but made Archie just sigh.
"Let me go do it Albie, Ill show the fucker."
Albie Leicester rubbed the head of his young brother and laughed.
"Now why would you want to risk getting that pretty face messed up Joey? Just be patient and your time will come. Archie get back round there and don't come back till you've either got the cash or a piece of that wanker as payment."
Doing as he was told Archie Leicester made his way back to the White Hart and by the time he arrived wasn't in the best of moods. This wasn't how he'd planned to spend his Friday night. He was supposed to be meeting Betty Woodcock who was always dying for a shag. Getting his leg over had been a bit scarce of late and now he was going to have to cancel the one chance he'd had in weeks. It was still warm and the doors were propped open. Peter Rathbone was now behind the counter and there were only a couple of locals in. In their seventies, Maurice Chambers and Arthur Farrow had been frequenting the White Hart since they were teenagers. They always sat quietly in a corner playing dominoes or crib and were never any trouble. Arthur eyed Archie suspiciously but when he stared long and hard at the man, Arthur soon

dropped his gaze. Everyone on the manor was only too aware of what the Leicester's were capable of and at his time of life Arthur Farrow wasn't about to bring trouble on himself. Quickly finishing up their pints, the two old men left the building. A game of fives and threes was only half over but at least they would live to play another day. Peter slowly shook his head when Archie walked up to the bar.
"Look Mr Leicester I aint being funny but I told you before I aint got the cash."
Archie pointed to the optics and Peter dutifully obliged the man and poured a double shot. Downing it in one Archie Leicester slammed the glass onto the bar and it shattered into several pieces. Selecting the largest shard Archie began to speak.
"Right then Petey boy what's it going to be?"
Peter Rathbone began to sweat and opening the till he hastily emptied its contents and pushed it across the bar.
"Honest Mr Leicester that's all I've got, I had to restock today."
Archie, still with the shard of glass in his hand, walked round to the other side of the bar and Peter backed into the shelves knocking a few glasses to the floor as he did so.
"Pleaseeeeee Mr Leicester pleaseeeeeeeeeeee."
"The pleading and begging were ignored and grabbing hold of Peter Rathbone's ear, Archie with one swift motion, sliced off the lobe and threw it on

to the bar. The screams were blood curdling but no one came to the man's rescue. Archie smiled as he admired his handy work. Blood oozed down Peter Rathbone's neck and changed the colour of his white shirt to crimson. Archie Leicester then scooped up the money and the piece of ear before making his way to the door.

"Now as I said before Petey boy, I'll be back in the morning for what's owed and god fucking help you if you aint got it."

Albie would be pleased with his work and taking back at least some cash and a piece of Petey boy would go down well. All in all it hadn't been a bad day's work and as it was he still had time to meet Betty.

The following day and just as he'd said, Archie Leicester made his way over to the White Hart. Accompanied by Fletch and Big Steve, two of the family's regular gang, Archie was ready for trouble. Word was already out on the manor about what had occurred the previous evening and many of the local landlords were up in arms. Just in case there was aggro Albie had told his brother to go mob handed. Walking along the high street they were met with many disapproving glances but people quickly lowered their heads when it looked like they might be confronted. The pub was deathly quiet and when Fletch rapped hard on the door there was no answer. Archie instructed Big Steve to force the door and when they got inside the place was deserted. The living quarters were in disarray and it appeared Peter Rathbone had left in a hurry. Archie smiled.

"Well lads it looks as if we've got ourselves a nice little gaff to add to the Leicester Empire."

Returning home with the news Archie was expecting a pat on the back from Albie but it wasn't forthcoming.

"A fucking pub! What the fuck do I want with a boozer?"

"I thought we could move the office, it might be good for business. There's a girl I know Betty Woodcock who could run it for us. A nice little piece of skirt if I do say so myself, she'd bring the punters in Albie."

"Yeah and the fucking Old Bill as well. Look I suppose you aint done that bad but I aint moving to no pub. Install the tart and we'll see how it goes but fucking gawd help her if she skims off the top."

And so the Leister family's reputation grew along with many diverse assets acquired along the way. Joey in recent months had started to become an embarrassment to Archie. The boy never seemed to lift a finger yet Albie could see no wrong in him. Hanging out most nights at the White Hart and never paying for a drink, he was really starting to piss Betty off. Warned in advance about skimming she was now on Archie's back every five minutes.

"Look Betty just because I fuck you now and again and you work for me don't give you the bleeding

right to bad mouth me brother."
In anger Betty threw the bar towel she'd been wiping up with into the sink and marched over to her on off boyfriend.
"I aint fucking bad mouthing the little tow rag but when Albie sees that the takings don't match the stock it'll be my fucking head on the block. Can't you see that?"
"Of course I can. Look leave it with me and Ill speak to him ok? Now come over here and give us a kiss."
Archie Leicester knew she was right and he would have a word with his little brother. He liked Betty and the last thing he wanted was for her to be on the receiving end of Albie's anger. It was just past nine when Archie reached home and found Joey alone in the kitchen.
"Where's Albie?"
"Seeing to a bit of business over in Bow."
"Well I'm glad you're on your own because I wanted to have a quiet word about the pub. Betty says you're drinking in there a lot and not paying your bill."
Joey Leicester flew into a rage and his lips seemed to snarl as he spoke.
"That fucking whore been telling tales has she? I'm going round there and sort the bitch out, you see if I don't."
With that Archie snapped. All the years, of putting up with Joey and not being able to say a word

because Albie told him not to, suddenly came flooding out. Grabbing his brother by the scruff of the neck Archie almost threw him onto the kitchen chair.

"Now you listen to me you little cunt! Touch one fucking hair on her head and I'll do for you I swear. I've just about had a gut full of you thinking you can do and say whatever you want without any repercussions. Do I make myself clear?"

Joey just smirked, causing his brother to tighten his grip.

"Well do I?"

Knowing that Archie wouldn't leave him alone until he answered, Joey Leicester gave just the hint of a nod but it was enough indication for his brother to release his grip.

Archie Leicester stormed from the room and slammed the door as he went. His action had made no impact on Joey and after straightening his clothes; he left the house and headed in the direction of the White Hart. Joey knew he had carte blanche to do as he liked. Archie wouldn't dare touch him as he was too scared of what Albie would do to him.

Since Peter Rathbone's departure the White Hart was always busy. Through fear the locals all drank in the pub at least once a week, whether they wanted to or not. Joey Leicester burst through the front door and stormed up to the bar. Betty had just finished serving a customer and when she turned round and saw who'd come in, was instantly filled with fear.

"Right you fucking whore! Been bad mouthing me have you?"

This was all Betty Woodcock needed but she was slightly comforted with the fact that Joey wouldn't really kick off while there was a pub full of punters. How wrong she was.

"Look Joey I...."

"You cunt! No one talks about me without paying the price, I think it's time you was taught a lesson." Swiftly he moved forwarded and head butted Betty Squarely between the eyes. Instantly she felt a crack as her nose broke and split open. Betty screamed out in pain but Joey still hadn't finished. Lunging at her cheek he bit down hard until his teeth met. As Joey stood back and with blood running from the corners of his mouth, he resembled a cannibal as he chewed on the piece of flesh then swallowed it. It was all done so matter of fact, there was no feeling or emotion and Joeys eyes were filled with a dark vengeance. An outright coward, he didn't hang about to admire the damage he'd caused and was out of the place as quickly as he'd entered. A couple of the regulars went to the aid of their land lady but a lot of damage had been done. Back then, there wasn't much on offer in the way of plastic surgery and what there was, seldom turned out to look very good. Doctors at the hospital did their best to close up the wound but with such a large piece of her cheek missing it still looked horrendous. With her face now permanently disfigured, Betty Woodcock discharger herself and rapidly disappeared from the area. Joey Leicester was never brought to book by either of his brothers. Albie, because he never punished his younger brother and Archie, well because without Betty to back up the story, then it was just hearsay. Fletch was installed at the white Hart in the hope that it would calm Joey down but it didn't work. One year later news reached Archie that Betty had been spotted in Soho plying her trade, the only option left open to her considering how she now looked. He felt sorry for the girl but there was little that Archie Leicester could do. Archie was under no illusion that his brother was evil but as he was so well protected, things were going to carry on just as always, unless there was someone else who had the guts to put him in his place. That situation would arise in the not too distant future and in the form of one Tony Segretti.

CHAPTER ELEVEN

Antonio Segretti was second generation Italian. His parents had moved to England in eighteen ninety four a year before Antonio's birth. The youngest of six he had continually fought for every scrap and morsel and that fact had made him the man he was today. Considered the black sheep by all but his mother, Antonio Segretti had left home by the age of fourteen and begun to call himself Tony. With gambling still illegal in England he had started off as a bookies runner. Tony would collect the tickets every hour from various establishments and then race round to Milky Thompsons house. Milky ran his illegal gambling from the back room of number three East Arbour Street. Johnny Thompson had been given the nickname Milky by his family years earlier. People assumed it was because his skin was so pale due to the fact that he never left the house. In reality he was an albino. Back then little was known of the condition and rather than be seen as a freak he'd happily taken the name of Milky on board.

The gambling trade was good and Tony would be paid a fee for each ticket he delivered. Soon he had accumulated a nice few quid, enough to start branching out in the business world on his own. Buying and selling, mostly stolen goods, was the order of the day and Tony Segretti excelled at it. By the time he'd reached twenty, world war one had been under way for a year but Tony was not patriotic and had no intention of fighting for his country. When it suited, Tony Segretti saw himself as Italian and when things were going good, then he was English through and through. As the war raged things got a little tight but he still managed to pay his rent and feed himself. Tony had dreams, dreams of being a someone but just how that would come to be, he couldn't have imagined in his wildest dreams.

When the war ended Tony was still only twenty three but was fast gaining a reputation for being a nasty piece of work. Standing six feet tall and with a mane of jet black hair he was almost perfect to look at. The only thing to spoil his handsome face was a five inch scar that ran horizontally down his right cheek. The disfigurement happened one night towards the end of nineteen seventeen. By then Tony had his own small crew, five young men who were all of a similar age to their boss and who hung on his every word. Like him they had all been dodging national service and they felt a sense of safety when they were all together. The six had been drinking at the Duke of Sussex pub over in Hackney when a man unknown to the group entered. Wanting to gain more credibility with his men, Tony had for no reason at all started a fight. His victim had seemed quite ill offensive and hadn't been looking for trouble. In fact a cold beer and maybe a small amount of banter was as much

entertainment as he was expecting that night. Tony Segretti wasn't aware that his mark was Mack Sewell a well known hard man who carried a deadly switch blade. Tony landed the first punch and Mack went straight down.
"What the fuck?"
As the punch came out of the blue Mack Sewell was stunned but he soon came to his senses. Laughter could be heard from Tony's men and as he raised his arms in a gesture of triumph, even more laughter erupted. Soaking up the admiration, he never saw Mack swiftly rise to his feet. Drawing the knife from his jacket, Mack flicked open the blade and grabbing Tony's arm, pulled him back round. In a split second Tony Segretti's right cheek was laid open and blood pumped freely from the wound. The place was in uproar with women screaming and Tony's crew trying to pick up their boss and stem the flow of blood. Nobody noticed that Mack Sewell had already made a quick escape. It had taken twenty stitches to sew up Tony's face and had left him with a permanent reminder, too in future choose his marks more carefully. The incident didn't go unlogged but it would take Tony Segretti a further two years to track down the man who had scared him for life and seek out his revenge.
Originally a butcher, Mack Sewell had earned his reputation as someone who could be hired if anyone had a spot of trouble. In the right circles his name was notorious for what he was capable off.

In everyday life he was just a normal geezer going about his business which is exactly what he'd been doing on the night Tony Segretti had attacked him for no reason. Mack Sewell took pride in his name but it was a name that would die along with its owner on the night of March the fifteenth nineteen twenty.

There was no big fight, no so called gang war, just Tony Segretti standing in a shop doorway with his own switch blade. Passersby screamed at the scene of a man lying on the pavement with blood pumping from a fatal wound. It was pitch black as Tony pulled up the collar of his overcoat and calmly walked away. No one ever knew who the culprit was, though many suspected but the revenge had never been about gaining kudos. Tony didn't let anyone get the better of him or if they did then they ultimately ended up paying the price.

Times were hard and even though it was two years after world war one, things were still in short supply. It hadn't stopped Tony moving forward and he now held court in a pub named The Crown and Two Chairman. Its location was close to where Peggy Spencer resided but it would be a further twenty one years before their paths would ever cross.

The Crown as it was shortened to, sat on the corner of Dean and St Andrews and was well known for being a den of iniquity and not frequented by anyone with good moral standards. Tony Segretti didn't own the pub but had moved in a year earlier via threats and intimidation, not too dissimilar to the Leicester's actions. The real gangster scene of the area wouldn't get under way until the mid nineteen fifties but Tony Segretti was still making a name for himself. If you wanted anything of an illegal nature then one of Tony's men, at a price, could supply it. The cost was usually exorbitant but no one dared to complain. It had begun with stolen property but had swiftly moved on to robbery, murder and the supply of a small amount of opium. It would be years away from the big drug deals of today but Tony still made a tidy profit from the few who required it. His supply was purchased from Wang Ho in China town and Tony could see that there was vast sums to be made. This wouldn't be the case for many years yet and long after his own death but sales had still grown in the short time that he was dealing. People were still suffering financial hardship. Not people of any standing but locals, hard working family people. There wasn't enough food and for most it was hand to mouth survival. Noticing the daily suffering gave Tony Segretti a business idea. He would loan the poor bastards a few coppers then charge an exorbitant rate of interest until the debt was repaid. It was the birth of the working class loan shark and to begin with many thought the infamous Mr Segretti was a fantastic man. That was until the first Friday after the initial loan, and then opinions changed drastically. Still, gluttons for punishment, people kept on borrowing. News of this young man's growing empire soon reached the ears of the Leicester family. Too lazy to start a similar venture themselves they decided to wait for the right moment and then just take Tony's. That would turn out to be a big mistake, resulting in their downfall and ultimate demise.

Never having felt threatened well at least not since the Mack Sewell incident, Tony often went out on collections alone. Joey Leicester had been instructed to follow the man then report back to his brothers. On this particular day Tony's collection was over in Stepney. It was only four miles from Soho but he didn't usually do much business outside of his own manor. The deciding factor had been that this was a big lend and one he couldn't turn down, so reluctantly he'd taken on the new client.

As usual Joey had ignored what he'd been told to do and on seeing Tony leave the debtors house, had followed him down the back alley of Steels Lane.

"Oi Geezer!"

Tony turned around but didn't recognise the man and felt no threat.

"Yeah?"

"Hand over your fucking money cunt!"

"Don't be a fucking knob mate, now get on your fucking bike and I'll let it go just this once."

Joey was becoming irate at being spoken to like a kid and his anger began to build into rage.

"I said hand over the fucking dosh!"
Tony Segretti laughed at the cheek of the man and ignoring him continued on his way. Suddenly he felt a hard blow to the back of his legs. Joey had concealed a small truncheon in the rear of his trousers. Tony fell to his knees and was momentarily stunned. Rolling onto his side, he saw Joey lunge forward with a wooden object which narrowly missed Tony's head. Now he was angry, adrenalin pumped through his veins and his heart was beating like crazy. Jumping to his feet Tony grappled the lead filled cosh from his assailant's hand. Breaking free, Joey, never one to enjoy a fair fight seized the opportunity to flee and turned to run. He hadn't got more than a few paces when Tony pulled back his arm and launched the cosh in the direction of Joeys head. With a loud crack the missile made contact with its target and Joey Leicester's body fell to the ground with a dull thud. Another resounding crack could be heard as Joey's forehead hit the cobbled alleyway. What had started out as a good day for Tony soon turned into a nightmare. He hadn't set out to kill anyone and now on the floor before him lay a dead man.
Back at the Crown Tony Segretti poured himself a large brandy; he was slightly shaken but relieved that no one had seen him. It wasn't until Barry Perrin, his right hand man, came running in to tell him that one of the Leicester brothers had been found dead down an alley, that anxiety began to set

in. The Leicester's knew very little about Tony Segretti but it wasn't likewise. Tony knew lots about the Leicester's and had heard of the horrific acts they'd carried out. Much was just rumour but a lot of it wasn't and he was well aware that there was no smoke without fire.

Back at Jamaica Street things were becoming crazy. Tempers were escalating and the air was thick with tension. The Leicester crew knew only too well what their boss was capable off and that things could quickly get out of hand, still not one of them had the guts to voice an opinion. Archie sat in a chair with his head in his hands but Albie was pacing the floor as he ranted over and over again.

"I'll kill the cunt slowly, tear him apart limb by fucking limb for what he's done."

Standing up, Archie tried to console his brother but they were just wasted words.

"Hang on a minute Albie, we aint sure it was Segretti."

Albie Leicester shoved his brother hard in the chest.

"Aint fucking sure it was him? What are you some sort of lily livered cunt! of course it was him and believe you me, if it's the last fucking thing I do on this earth Ill make sure he pays."

Tony Segretti already knew what would happen and not wanting a full scale war he went into hiding. He was well aware that the brothers would never rest until he was dead but space and time would allow him the element of surprise. A week after the murder Joey Leicester's funeral was held. All locals were expected to attend and god help them if they didn't. Mixing in with the crowd and wearing a flat cap with his coat collar turned up as high as it would go, Tony watched the procession. Every hard man, bank robber and Brass was there; in fact anyone from the criminal fraternity in the whole of the Smoke had turned up.

Over the next two weeks and always well hidden by the shadows, Tony followed the brothers every movement. This wouldn't be war, what he needed to do would be carried out in a cold, calculated and calm fashion. It was kill or be killed and Tony knew that he would only get one chance.

Information was given that Archie Leicester was more than fond of a bit of skirt, so out of the two brothers he would be the easiest to take. Tony discovered that the man's preference for sex was always on a Friday night. With this insight to hand he followed his mark to the Blind Beggar pub on Whitechapel Road. It was common knowledge that Archie liked girls who were a bit on the plump side and Annie Rayner was all that he'd hoped for. A traditional sing song was taking place and the pub was packed to capacity. When Archie walked in the crowd parted like the red sea and he made his way over to his so called date. After a quick hello, the pair were soon bumping and grinding in the pubs back yard. Archie was concentrating hard on the task in hand and didn't hear his assailant approach.

Tony crept along the outer wall and luckily for him Annie Rayner had her eyes closed as she groaned in pleasure. It wouldn't have been a problem if she'd seen him but he was glad that he wouldn't have to take an innocent life. Removing a large bayonet from inside his coat, Tony raised himself up onto the balls of his feet. This motion allowed him to extend the steel blade high above his head. Archie Leicester was too engrossed with the matter in hand to notice anything as he greedily sucked and slurped on Annie's neck. With one swift movement Tony plunged the blade down through Archie's shoulder and deep into his chest. The top of Archie Leicester's heart was pierced and even though he managed to let out a groan, by the time Annie Raynor began to scream, he was already dead. After swiftly retracting his weapon Tony didn't hang around and had scaled the back wall, pulled up the collar of his coat and was now disappearing down the street. Again he did his vanishing act for a couple of weeks and waited until Archie's funeral was over. All the while Albie Leicester was going mad, eaten up with anger and rage. Daily he sent his crew out looking for Tony but they always drew a blank. The Crown was ransacked and a few of Tony's men were severely beaten and hospitalized. Their pleas for mercy fell on deaf ears but not one of them was able to shed any light as to where their boss was. Albie had stepped up security and as Tony monitored his movements, he soon found out that the man was never alone. Accepting that there would now be more than one casualty he mentally formed a plan.

Sunday mornings were spent at the cemetery. Albie Leicester would first visit his parent's grave, then move on to Archie's. Finally he ended his visit at young Joeys and his time spent there was always in tears. To avoid embarrassment, Albie's escort big Bert Marsden would sit in a small pavilion at the rear of the cemetery. He was close enough to keep an eye on his boss but far enough away to give Albie some privacy.

Tony decided to go for the minder first and carrying a bunch of flowers that concealed a claw hammer, he walked towards the pavilion. Smiling at Bert he tipped his hat.

"Excuse me Sir; I'm looking for the grave of Mrs Peterfield."

Bert Marsden relaxed and was about to tell the man he couldn't help him when Tony quickly pulled out the hammer and smashed it down squarely on top of Bert's head. The force was so strong that it actually imbedded in the man's skull and Tony had to pull hard to release the hammer. Bert Marsden died instantly. As his large frame slumped to the round it was a relief to Tony, Bert was huge and in a struggle he knew he wouldn't have stood much of a chance. Using Bert's coat lapel he wiped the claw hammer clean of brain tissue.

Albie Leicester was kneeling beside Joeys grave

sobbing. He didn't hear Tony Segretti approach but even if he had he wouldn't have stood a chance. Tony rained down blow after blow on Archie Leicester's skull. Far more than was needed but he wasn't taking any chances that the man could recover. With each blow skin and hair flapped about and by the time he'd finished, Albie Leicester had little of his skull left.

When the Leicester Empire ended there was bedlam on the streets of the east end. It took a month for things to at last quieten down. The Crown was refurbished and soon Tony Segretti was approached by most of the Leicester crew. They all wanted jobs and swore their allegiance to Tony. Feeling it was better the devil he knew, each was taken on but not once did Tony Segretti ever trust them or let his guard down. His philosophy of keeping his friends close and his enemies even closer would over the years pay off in many ways.

The events of the last few weeks would shape Tony into the man that he would become, cold, calculating and with no respect or compassion for anyone.

CHAPTER TWELVE
WAR TORN LONDON 1941

Peggy Spencer had been on the game for almost twenty five years. Now in her late forties her choice of lifestyle was really starting to take its toll. She seemed so tired all the time and getting out of bed each day was becoming a chore. Money was in short supply but there always seemed to be a bill to pay and Peggy had noticed of late, that even the men who were out of their heads on drink seemed to be avoiding her. It was getting tougher and tougher to make a living as a brass and the war wasn't helping matters. Peggy had first thought that the influx of soldiers into the capital would greatly increase business but that hadn't been the case. The younger brasses were doing all the business of late and any past forty really seemed to be struggling. Never a natural beauty to look at, Peggy had for a long time, been able to maintain her hour glass figure. A small waist and ample breasts had always secured her plenty of work but as the years passed Peggy's waist had expanded and her breasts had begun to sag. Now even the sex starved Tommy's on leave from the war didn't seem to give her a second glance. It had all been so different in the beginning but that was back in the early nineteen twenties.
Twenty five years earlier Peggy had been so desperate to escape the clutches of her overbearing

mother that she left her home and headed for the city never to return. On her first attempt she managed to land employment in a typing pool. Peggy would be the first to admit it wasn't the most glamorous of jobs but at least it paid the bills. Since moving to London from Middlesex three weeks earlier, her small amount of savings had dwindled fast. News of her employment had been like music to her ears and she was up with the larks on the first day. By the end of her shift Peggy realised that it was going to be a mind numbing, soul destroying profession and thought that there must be something better on offer elsewhere. Peggy Spencer completed her first week but didn't feel any better about things, even when she was handed her wage packet. Take home pay was just a few shillings and by the time she paid for rent and food there wasn't much left over. Still she was able to put aside enough for a couple of glasses of Gin.

It was a Friday night and leaving straight after work she'd headed to Soho in the hope of meeting a rich young man. Her office was situated on Charing Cross road so she only had to turn left into Villiers Street and she was bang in the middle of what real life was all about, finding excitement and having fun. In the Nineteen twenties the Soho area was a cosmopolitan melting pot of Italians, Greeks, Jews from Eastern Europe and any other breed of human being from every corner of the world that you could think of. Restaurants, cafes and shops all selling

foreign provisions filled the streets and jostled for competition with the many bars and clubs that had begun to open. It was a new age; the first war had been over for almost seven years and after all the heart break and hardship, people wanted excitement. Peggy's first port of call was a place called The Hotel De France. Slightly naive she may have been but Peggy was a quick learner and after several minutes of listening to the conversation of smart young men with baby soft skin, she realised that this establishment was for Gay men only. Although against the law, homosexuality much to Peggy's disgust was starting to be openly flaunted in Soho.   Desperate to find a companion Peggy moved on to The Hungry Horse pub but this was as bad as the last place and reluctantly Peggy decided to give up and go home. All she'd wanted was a drink to relieve her stress and some nice conversation that could possibly lead to more. Her mother had continually berated her and it was the main reason Peggy had left home in the first place.
"Peggy Spencer! You'll never get a man as long as you have a bleeding hole in your arse."
Determined to prove her mother wrong, Peggy had moved the short distance from Harefield to the city but now with her head hung low, she walked along and contemplated spending another night alone in her room. Not looking where she was going, Peggy was almost knocked over as she walked straight into a stranger.

"I'm so sorry my dear, are you alright?"
Peggy Spencer smoothed down her dress and hair and then pouted her lips in a provocative manner.
"I'm fine thank you very much."
She had only taken a few steps further when the stranger spoke again.
"Excuse me Miss but could I buy you a drink"
Peggy's face beamed back at the man and she coyly nodded her head.
"I'm David by the way; David Millroy and I work over in Whitehall."
Peggy thought she'd hit the jack pot and eagerly introduced herself.
"Peggy, Peggy Spencer. Pleased to make your acquaintance Mr Millroy I'm sure."
"Please call me David. Now where would you like me to take you Miss Spencer?"
Peggy relayed the places she had already been to and mimicked the type that frequented them, which had her escort in stitches of laughter. "Well I'm sure we can do better than that."
Linking his arm in hers David Millroy led Peggy along the street.
"I know a charming establishment called The Bonnington Hotel. It's only a short walk from here and it would be an honour if you would join me."
Although nervous it didn't stop Peggy and once outside it at last registered with her what this particular gentleman was after. At first the idea of being labelled a prostitute didn't sit well with her

but the bills had to be paid and she could think of worse things than receiving money for something she enjoyed. Peggy had always been promiscuous, it was more by luck than judgement that she hadn't already got pregnant and she hoped that tonight Lady Luck would still be with her.

The hotel was newly built and its decor and furnishings were the height of fashion. The staff were polite, even though they were aware of the fact, that at times it was frequented by prostitutes. It wasn't something that the manager liked to encourage but times were hard and he wasn't about to turn away the business just because it was immoral.

After the couple had consumed several drinks David Millroy walked over to the reception area and booked a room. An hour later and when the deed had been done Peggy smoothed down her dress and held out her hand. David Millroy hadn't until now been sure if his companion was on the game, or if she was just a young girl out for fun. Now that she'd indicated payment was required he was a little relieved that there wasn't going to be any misunderstanding. Smiling he handed over a five pound note.

"I take it you don't do much business in this neck of the woods then Peggy?"

Peggy Spencer laughed out loud.

"To be honest love this is my first trick but it won't be me bleeding last I can tell you. There's no way

I'm going back to that shit hole of a typing pool again, not when I can get paid for doing something I like."

True to her word Peggy Spencer never returned to the typing pool. Soon she left her lodgings and moved into a cosy one bedroom flat just off old Compton Street in Soho. It didn't take her long to get into the swing of things and learning to read the signs of a good punter or one to avoid became second nature. Time passed quickly and for many years trade had been good but as Peggy aged her clientele dwindled. Now here in nineteen forty one with a war raging across Europe she was in dire straits. The gay community had begun to take over the area and it deterred the married men from seeking out the company of a Tom. The police would do sporadic raids at various venues and when this did occur, it seemed as if the whole place closed ranks. No one would ever testify so it was almost impossible to get a conviction and as the war worsened, these raids became less frequent. Peggy Spencer was now overweight and every line on her face seemed to become more prominent by the day. Nothing she tried improved her situation but still, night after night she ventured onto the dark streets with the hope of selling her body.

On one of her so called quiet nights, something that was becoming more and more of the norm, Peggy took some time to monitor her surroundings. She also noted the practices of the other working girls who were also plying their trade on the street. Suddenly she could see something that had been staring her in the face but until now she'd took no notice of. There were five Toms on Dean Street that evening. Three were in their early twenties but the other two by Peggy's estimation were no more than fifteen and it was these two that were doing the most business. Not marginally more business but considerably more. No sooner had one of them returned from some dark alley with a punter than she was immediately in demand again. The scenario was never ending and Peggy didn't need to see the cash changing hands to know that these girls were making a mint. Transfixed she stood and watched for a good two hours. The girl's clients, who were mostly Tommy's and still in their uniforms, definitely liked them young. Peggy had to accept her time on the game was fast coming to an end but fortunately for her she had come up with a good idea. Putting it into practice was another matter and she knew she would need help. It had always been her rule to live a solitary existence and not to draw attention to herself. Peggy had avoided pimps like the plague and the gangsters in Soho had been a definite taboo area but needs must and times were hard, so Peggy Spencer decided to do the one thing she'd always sworn she wouldn't, ask for the help of a man. Deciding to call it a night Peggy hadn't got more than a few hundred yards when she spotted a smartly dressed young girl leaning

against a wall. About to pass by she noticed that the girl was crying. It wasn't out of the ordinary to see a woman in tears, not here in Soho anyway but this girl looked different from the Brasses that normally loitered the streets. Peggy didn't have a maternal bone in her body and it was more a case of being nosy than anything else that made her stop. For a start this young girl was absolutely stunning. Tall and with a mane of raven black hair she looked out of place. If Peggy had wanted to be over critical she could have said that the girl's nose was a tad on the large side but somehow it seemed to add to her beauty.
"Hey there love! Things can't be that bad can they?"
Esther Goldman lifted her head and sniffed loudly. Her bottom lip quivered as she began to speak.
"I'm lost."
"Where are you trying to get to love?"
"Home!"
The girl's one word answer and reluctance to give any information was making Peggy agitated but at the same time she didn't want to miss out on an opportunity. This girl was pretty and could just turn out to be the first piece in her jigsaw.
"Look, how about I take you for a nice cup of rosie and you can tell me all about it. Things are rarely as bad as they seem. Now my flats just around the corner or we could stop at Jims Cafe which is just over there. Esther Goldman eyed Peggy with

suspicion as she looked her up and down. After a few seconds she decided it would be safer in a public place and she was so hungry and thirsty.
"Can we go to the cafe please?"
Peggy smiled and gently holding the girls arm steered her across the road. Once they were seated and had a warm drink in front of them, Peggy again asked the girl where it was she wanted to go. "I live on Bell Lane just behind Petticoat Lane."
 "You really are off the beaten track that must be a good three or four miles away."
"Three and a half actually."
Peggy Spencer laughed out loud. About to inquire further, she was halted when Esther began to speak. Once she started there was no stopping her and as each sentence ended with a fresh onslaught of tears, Peggy became more and more interested.
"I got news today that my parents have been killed in a blast over in Golders Green. They went to visit friends last night and as they were walking back to their car the Luftwaffe dropped a bomb. When they hadn't returned this morning I went looking for them and a Rabbi who saw the whole thing from down the street, said they didn't stand a chance."
More tears erupted and Peggy fished a handkerchief from her bag and handed it to the girl.
"So how'd you end up in Soho love?"
"Don't know really. I just started walking and before I knew where I was I ended up here."
Peggy was becoming more and more interested in

young Esther Goldman. She wanted to rub her hands together but thought better than to count her chickens at this early stage.

"Wont there be anyone at home whose missing you?"

"No I'm an only child and what was left of my family back in Germany, recently perished at the hands of Hitler."

"Oh how awful!"

"When the first war started in nineteen fourteen my mother and father who were then only twenty thought it would be best if they came to England. For years my parents struggled with the English language and only managed to get by because my father's family were wealthy."

Peggy eyes momentarily opened wide but the look of greed went unnoticed to Esther.

"They were older when I came along, my mother always said I was a beautiful surprise, anyway once my schooling began, I sort of ended up being their translator. My relatives back in Germany were some of the first casualties of this new war and soon all that was left of the Goldman's, was our little family here in London. We were so close and spent all of our time together and now......."

A fresh onslaught of tears began and Peggy who was less agitated now, smiled tenderly at the girl.

"So this house on?"

"Bell Lane."

"Bell Lane that's right, so this house is it rented?"

"No my father bought it for my mother, it was one of the first things he did when they arrived here."
"Is it a big house love?"
Esther suspiciously narrowed her eyes; this woman did seem to be asking a lot of questions.
"Quite big I suppose, it's got three storeys and a basement. Why?"
"Oh, no reason love just making conversation."
Peggy Spencer had pound signs flashing before her eyes. Tenderly she stroked the young girls arm and with her most caring smile made Esther an offer, she was sure the girl in her upset state, wouldn't refuse.
"Well my dear Esther, I don't think you should be alone right now. Why don't you come and stay with me for a few days. My place aint very big but it's warm and safe and right at this minute I think that's what you need."
Esther Goldman mulled over the offer for a moment. The idea of going back to an empty house scared her and on the whole this lady seemed nice and kind. Esther tried to imagine what her mother would say and quickly settled on the notion that her mother would approve. In reality Mrs Goldman would have read the signals and told her daughter to run as fast as she could but Esther was so afraid and grieving that she didn't want to read the situation that way. So with a nod of her head the invitation was accepted and Peggy's idea of earlier was looking as though it might actually materialize.

First thing in the morning she would pay a visit to the main man, a man she was scared to death of but the one person who could put her plans into action and really get things up and running.

CHAPTER THIRTEEN

Well Billy boy that's all I know about them blokes early lives but I......."

"Dulcie as interesting as it is, what's any of that got to do with the bodies?"

"All in good time. Now I told you a little bit about Peggy but not enough for you to understand what happened and why. The next part is about me, Esther and poor old Peggy. Her beginnings came straight from the horse's mouth so I know that what I told you was true but as for the others, well I aint so sure. People always like to add a little bit on, makes it more exciting I suppose."

"Dulcie Please!"

"Ok ok, right then. I was born in Shepherds Bush back in nineteen twenty seven. The only child of John and Rita Gray to be precise. I suppose to begin with my childhood was really good, cosy and warm if you know what I mean. Dad had a good job, we weren't rich not by any standards but we didn't go without much. My mum looked after the house and all in all we was a happy little family. Anyway the year war broke out everything seemed to change, change overnight in fact. My Dad joined up, the navy to be exact and me and my mum would wait everyday for news. By the end of nineteen forty one that news came in the worst bleeding way possible. I remember me Mum had been hanging out the washing and I was glued to the radio as usual.

The knock at the door made me jump and as Mum didn't hear it I opened up."
Suddenly Dulcie Gray was back in nineteen forty one, November to be exact and the weather was bitterly cold.
"Can I help you mister?"
The two men stood on the door step; both dressed in naval uniforms and under the circumstances gave their best smile to the young girl.
"Is your Mum in Miss?"
"She's out the back and boy will she be pleased to see you, got some good news about me Dad have you?"
Neither of the men answered Dulcie's question as she showed them into the living room.
"Make yourselves at home and Ill fetch me mum."
Dulcie ran into the back yard yelling as she went.
"Quick Mum! quick, the men are here and they've got news on my dad."
Rita Gray dropped the basket of laundry she was holding and for a moment stood open mouthed. Unlike her child she was well aware of what the men were about to tell her and it wasn't going to be good. Walking towards the back door Rita made the sign of the cross and prayed that it was an injury and nothing worse. Dulcie saw the colour had drained from her mother's face and this image along with the cold breath escaping from her mouth had stayed with Dulcie for the whole of her life. It's funny what the brain chooses to make a lasting

impact on and for Dulcie it was this vision and nothing else that came to mind whenever she pictured her mother.

Under protest Dulcie was sent to her room but it wasn't more than a couple of minutes before she heard the shrill screams of Rita Gray. Descending the stairs in record time, she burst into the front room. Dulcie stopped dead in her tracks at the sight before her. One of the men was trying to comfort Rita who was draped over the side of the sofa sobbing her heart out. Dulcie ran over and flung her arms around Rita but her mother was having none of it and roughly pushed her daughter to one side. When the second man bent low and offered Rita a glass of brandy that he'd helped himself to from the sideboard, her mother smiled and happily accepted the drink. Since her father's death the months seemed to pass quickly and it was soon the spring of nineteen forty one. Dulcie Grays fourteenth birthday was fast approaching but she wasn't looking forward to it. Rita had changed since that fateful day when the news had arrived and it wasn't for the better. Days were spent laying around in her housecoat drinking gin. The place didn't get cleaned and on more than one occasion Dulcie went to bed hungry. Many times young Dulcie Gray would wake after a bad dream and search for her mother but the house was always empty. Rita now liked to go out dancing, it was something unheard of when Dulcie's father was alive but now her mother could please herself, she took full advantage of anything that was on offer. Things started to come to a head on the one and only night that Rita took a man back to the house. Dulcie had been told to sit quietly in the kitchen but she peered through a crack in the door and watched as Rita answered the front door. Her mother's hair had been dyed a bright brunette colour and was now piled high on her head. Her mouth shone with a shade of ruby red lipstick that Dulcie didn't care for. In fact lately Dulcie didn't care for anything about her mother and she knew that her dad would have gone up the wall if he'd seen what Rita was wearing. The blue satin wrap over dress pulled at every seam and Dulcie would swear that she could see her mother's breasts as they fought to escape from the low cut neck line.

"Hi Arty come on in. I've got some really good scotch; it'll help us relax as we get to know each other."

Dulcie screwed up her eyes as she scrutinised the visitor. He was tall and wore a loud type of suit. His hair was slicked back and she just sensed that he wasn't a nice man. Rita and her guest disappeared into the living room and it was only a few minutes later that giggling and moaning could be heard.

"Oh yes Arty that's gooooood. Oh you are a naughty man."

Dulcie didn't like what she was hearing, she wanted

to barge in and tell the man to leave her mum alone but she knew that if she did Rita would give her a right back hander. How her mother had changed in such a short time really upset Dulcie. Rita had once been a loving kind parent and in the past the house was always clean, filled with laughter and good food. Dulcie wished with all her heart that her Dad was here now; he would have known what to do. She decided to read her favourite book The Little White Horse it told the story of an orphaned girl who went to live with her cousin in a beautiful house. Beginning to daydream and that was all it would ever be as she had no other family but Rita; Dulcie suddenly looked up to find Arty Drew staring down at her. His breath smelled stale from the whisky and as he reached out to touch her Dulcie shrank back against the hard kitchen chair. "Fuck off and leave me alone!"

To Arty Drew it appeared that the youngster had a dirty mouth and he liked that a lot.

Her fear didn't seem to faze him and as he forced his hand up her dress, Dulcie screamed out. The noise brought her mother into the kitchen but instead of telling Arty to get out, Rita placed a hand gently on his arm.

"Come on lover you don't want scragg end when you've got a bit of prime fillet waiting for you." They both laughed out loud before disappearing back into the living room. Alone at the kitchen table, Dulcie sobbed until she felt there were no

more tears left. After half an hour and with no sign of her mother Dulcie decided that she might as well go to her room. Tiptoeing along the hall she stopped at the front room door. Slightly ajar Dulcie pressed her nose close to the gap and peered inside. Rita was leaning over the side of the armchair and Arty was behind her which blocked Dulcie's view. She opened her mouth with shock when she noticed her mother's cami knickers lying on the floor. Even though the light was dim Dulcie could see that Rita still had on her stockings and suspenders. When a passing cars head lamps momentarily shone through the window Dulcie saw Arty's bare buttocks and a sideways glance at her mother's breasts as they jiggled up and down. Arty Drew started to move backwards and forwards and then suddenly he grabbed a handful of Rita's hair and pulled her head backwards.
"Oh Art! Talk dirty to me you know I love it."
"You dirty bitch I'm going to fuck you hard, you like it hard don't you. You're a slut Rita Gray, a dirty fucking whore."
"Oh yes, oh yes Arty do it to me."
All of a sudden Arty Drew began to slap Rita's buttocks, all the while he was moving faster and faster and grunting out loud. Dulcie thought the sound was strange and began to giggle. The laughter alerted Rita and she stared at the door.
"If that's you Dulcie Gray you'd better fuck off right now, or you'll feel the back of my bleeding hand

and no mistake!"

Dulcie didn't need to be told twice and scarpered to her room praying that Rita would soon forget about the incident. Unlike today, girls of Dulcie's age were far more childlike and the more she thought about what she'd seen, the more it played on her mind. The experience of actually seeing her mother have sex brought a hardness to Dulcie Gray and she soon learned to look after herself, emotionally at least. There was one particular encounter with Mary Gibbins that resulted in a fight. Dulcie had to be pulled off of the girl and she soon found herself in the head mistresses office.

Mary was a chubby girl with a mane of ginger frizzy hair. Her freckles and round over sized horn rimmed glasses did nothing to enhance her looks but it wasn't just her outward appearance that was unappealing. Mary Gibbins was a bully, nothing more and nothing less and to add insult to injury she was also the teacher's pet. It was no surprise that it was Dulcie who got the blame when the girl ran in crying with a bloody nose.

"Well Miss Gray! What do you have to say for yourself and it had better be good or a letter will be going to your mother."

"Won't make a lot of difference, she's pissed most of the time so she wouldn't be able to read it anyway."

"Dulcie Gray! I should wash your mouth out with soap."

Dulcie knew she had over stepped the mark but she

was so fed up with everyone putting her down, it felt like she was totally alone in the world.

"Look Miss Burrows, Mary said me old lady was a good time girl. I aint got a bleeding clue what that means but I know it aint right. Would you let someone call your old lady a good time girl?"

"Now that is enough Dulcie! Go back to the classroom. I will deal with you later and I don't wish to hear another swear word pass your lips for the remainder of the day!"

The rest of the day passed without event and Dulcie really didn't think that anything more would happen regarding her behaviour but when she reached her street a strange car was parked outside. She prayed it wasn't Arty Drew again but when she walked in and saw a policeman sitting at the kitchen table, knew she would have been better off if it had been Arty. PC Jackson, the local bobby wasn't alone. Sitting with him was Rita and a strange lady, who said she was from the Women's Institute and was there to lend moral support or something. Dulcie didn't know what that meant but she didn't like the sound of it all the same. Rita stood up, walked over to her daughter and swiftly slapped Dulcie's face. The woman from the Women's Institute gasped in horror.

"Mrs Gray! There will be no need for that sort of carry on."

Rita was about to give the woman a piece of her mind for poking her nose into affairs that didn't

concern her but then thought better of it. Instead she led Dulcie to a chair and forced her to sit down.
"Now then my girl, it's been brought to my attention that you've been fucking acting up at school. Well I aint having it Dulcie do you hear? These people want you to be an evacuee and I think it's a good idea."
Dulcie, still rubbing at her tingling cheek, looked at each person in the room as she asked.
"What's an evacuee?"
Rita didn't reply and only looked towards the policeman in a silence that told him she would rather he answered the question.
"An evacuee young lady is someone, though mostly children at the moment, who are moved to rural areas and stay with other families. It's just until the war is over and there are no more threats of bombings.
Dulcie didn't need it explaining again and within minutes she had raced up the stairs, threw a few things into her small leather suitcase and was again standing in the kitchen. This wouldn't be the beautiful house like in her story but as far as she was concerned it was the next best thing. Rita Gray now stood at the kitchen sink smoking a cigarette.
"Well fuck my old boots you ungrateful little bitch. I'll tell you something for nothing my girl. I just might not want you back after this bleeding war ends."
Dulcie didn't think that was a bad idea and as she

followed the bobby and the strange lady out of the house, she didn't even give her mother a kiss goodbye.

There were many people at Kings Cross station and they were mostly children with their parents hugging and kissing them. As Dulcie stood alone on the platform she scanned the area looking for someone her own age as all of the evacuees were under ten and she felt a bit strange. A woman approached and handed her a piece of cardboard with Dulcie's name written on it. Everything was confusing and Dulcie didn't have a clue what was going on.

"Tie this bit of string on dearie and hang it round your neck."

"Why?"

"Case you get lost darling, now don't look so worried all the kids have them."

Dulcie Gray thought it was a stupid idea but dutifully did as she was told and then boarded the train for her journey. It would be an exciting adventure and one Dulcie was looking forward too. Five hours later and the train pulled up into the small station at Kirkby Stephen. It was a far cry from Kings Cross and as Dulcie along with the legion of other children disembarked, she stood on the platform not knowing what to do next. It was past nine o'clock, dark and Dulcie Gray was scared. Suddenly she could hear her name being called. A man and woman who appeared to be in their mid fifties stood at the far end of the only platform to service the town.

"Come here girl and stop dallying about."

The none too friendly words were spoken from the man and he looked mean. Suddenly Dulcie thought this wasn't such a good idea and that maybe she'd jumped out of the frying pan and into the fire. The woman's hair was prematurely gray and her face was lined and tired looking. As Dulcie approached the couple the man turned and strutted towards a large Ford Van. The woman who Dulcie would later have to call Mrs Dobson followed close behind with her head bent low. Opening up the back door, Bert Dobson told Dulcie to get inside before climbing into the cab alongside his wife. They must have travelled for a good three or four miles down country tracks and all the time Dulcie Gray was being thrown from one side of the vehicle to the other. Finally they screeched to a halt and the doors were once more opened. There would have been plenty of room for all three to travel up front but instead Dulcie had been treated as if she were cattle. Outside it was pitch black and the surroundings couldn't really be made out, though Dulcie did wrinkle her nose up at the smell, which she would later find out was pigs shit.

"Right you! Get in that barn and stay there till morning. If you dare to venture out, the missus or I will come to get you, then a good thrashing will be in order. Do you hear?"

Dulcie could only look in horror and when she didn't speak, Bert Dobson moved so close to her that Dulcie thought he would knock her over.

"I said! Do you hear?"

"Yes I heard you, fuck me!"

"What did you just say?"

Dulcie knew she was in for it, she really had to cut back on the bad language or it was going to get her in deep trouble.

"I said lucky me, what a wonderful gaff."

The farmer didn't understand half what the girl was saying and just shook his head.

Pulling open a latch door that creaked as it moved, Dulcie was handed a kerosene lamp and a box of matches. The door was then slammed shut behind her. Wind whistled through the numerous cracks and after Dulcie had managed to light the lamp she shone it around to look at her accommodation.

Dulcie Gray thought she had come to the end of the earth. A small bed had been made up in one corner but it didn't look inviting. Apart from a bowl and a jug of cold water that sat precariously on top of some kind of crate, the rest of the barn was barren. Climbing onto the bed Dulcie could feel the itchiness of the only blanket that had been left for her and she pulled the collar of her coat tightly around her neck. Instead of the wonderful adventure she had been hoping for, Dulcie realised she had come to hell on earth. Laying down her head, she prayed that things would look a little brighter in the morning.

CHAPTER FOURTEEN

It was nineteen forty one and Peggy Spencer's first encounter with the man who would set her on the way to large sums of money and an early retirement, or so she thought.
Peggy hadn't got much sleep having spent most of the night consoling Esther. In the small hours it had felt like the girl could cry for England. It wasn't that fact that Peggy was uncompassionate but not having been close to her own mother she couldn't understand why Esther was carrying on so. Finally the girl had drifted off to sleep and Peggy was able to get washed and dressed. Leaving a note Peggy had explained that she must attend a business meeting and that Esther could help herself to breakfast then wait until she returned. Esther Goldman was so very upset and when she woke and read the note was just glad that there was someone looking out for her.
Walking along Dean Street Peggy had been mentally preparing herself and mulling over what she was going to say but now about to put her plan into action, she could feel a kind of nervous nausea starting to build in the pit of her stomach. At last she was standing outside the Crown but now Peggy was hesitant about even entering the place. Over the years she'd heard all sorts of rumours regarding the man she was about to meet and was more than a

little scared. Still if she wanted to continue with her plan, then Tony Segretti or someone like him was what she needed, even if it went against the grain in every conceivable way. Pushing open one of the double doors Peggy entered. The place smelled heavily of tobacco and stale beer but much to her surprise appeared relatively clean. The bar seemed to be deserted until she spotted a grey haired man who was clearing away glasses. He momentarily glanced in her direction before resuming his duties. Peggy began to shake but she didn't know why and for a second contemplated cancelling her unscheduled appointment. Never one to give in, she silently chastised herself and then marched over to the pot man.

"Excuse me, could you tell me where I could find Tony Segretti?"

Stan Everett placed a glass back on the table and eyed the woman up and down. He'd worked at the Crown for years, seen many landlords come and go but Tony Segretti was a different kettle of fish altogether. The woman standing before him was a Brass there was no doubting that fact. It wasn't what she was wearing or the amount of makeup she had on but there was just something about a Tom if you knew what to look for. Still this woman was polite, had done him no harm and Stan wanted to warn her off.

"Are you sure you want Mr Segretti?"

Stan Everett wouldn't dare bad mouth his boss but

his facial expression said it all and Peggy was well used to reading people.

"Yes please."

After inviting Peggy to take a seat Stan climbed the stairs to the first floor office.

Alone in the bar Peggy. surveyed looked all around. She supposed the man hadn't done too bad for himself but on the other hand, given his reputation, couldn't understand why he at least hadn't moved on from this part of the Smoke. Still she reasoned it wasn't for her to judge and if he helped her then she didn't give a toss how he lived, how he spent his money or where he chose to reside. It took several seconds before Stan Everett was invited in and all the while he waited, Stan puffed out his cheeks in nervousness.

"There's a woman down stairs governor, says she'd like to see you. I aint sure but I think she might be a Tom."

"I've told you before not to refer to them as Toms. They can be the dirtiest bitches on the planet but when they come to me you treat them like ladies, understood?"

Tony Segretti stared hard at the old man and to Stan it felt as though Tony could read his every thought. Of course that wasn't the case but all the same his boss had a way of making people feel like that.

Tony sighed heavily.

"Show her up then."

Tony Segretti was no fool and much of his money

had been earned from the brasses of Soho. His Italian upbringing had taught him only one thing but that one thing had stood him in good stead over the years. Respect other people, even when you are knocking seven bells out of them, you still show respect.

Stan went back and beckoned for her to join him. This would all end in tears but what could he do except say run for your fucking life, not if he valued his own. Peggy followed the pot man back up the stairs and as he placed a hand on the door knob he whispered Be careful.

The office as everyone referred to it, looked more like someone's living room. Peggy found the bold floral paper a strange choice for a man with such a violent reputation. Pretty chintz curtains hung from the windows and were only spoilt by the blackout tape that covered the glass. Three over stuffed sofas filled the room and on a small table sat an elegant silver tea set. All in all it resembled the room of some high class hooker and for a moment Peggy smiled to herself.

Tony Segretti didn't speak but looked her up and down as if he was buying another piece of furniture and Peggy didn't like it. She was about to give him a mouthful of abuse when the man at last spoke.
"So Miss?"
"Spencer, Peggy Spencer."
"So Miss Spencer how can I help you."
Tony Segretti knew that whatever the woman

wanted it wasn't to ask for a job as one of his Toms. She was too old and from the lines on her face had entertained way too many men over the years. Still he would listen; he'd learnt early on that opportunities came in all shapes and sizes.

"I aint going to beat about the bush Mr Segretti, I need some help with a little business venture I'm planning and I thought of you. I know you're a busy man but if you could just spare me half an hour I can guarantee that you won't be disappointed."

Tony laughed in a way that seemed to Peggy as if he was mocking her. It wasn't the case but her nerves were getting the better of her and she was beginning to see things that were not even there. As infuriated as she was, Peggy wouldn't let him know how he was making her feel. Instead, she calmed herself, took a deep breath and carried on with what she'd come to say.

"I suppose you know I'm a Brass?"

Tony just smiled, he wasn't about to be rude and waved his hand in a gesture that said 'It's of no interest to me so just continue'.

"Well recently my business has begun to decline, drastically in fact. Even this bastard war hasn't improved things. The Tommy's are more particular than your average fucking Joe, so a woman of my age aint got much of a chance. At least not when I'm up against women or should I say girls, that are young enough to be me daughters. Anyway I've

been watching the local Toms and the ones doing any real trade are young and I mean young."
"And where exactly do I come into all this?"
Tony Segretti could recognise a good business opportunity when he saw one and beckoned with his hand for Peggy to take a seat. He already had several young brasses working for him, so whatever this Peggy Spencer was offering had to be a bit special.
"I recently made the acquaintance of a young girl, comes from money actually. In the last couple of days her poor old mum and dad got killed in a bombing. Bleeding sad I know but them's the times we live in. Anyway seems this youngster has a house and a big one at that. Poor little fucker aint got no family and no one to take care of her."
When she reached her last sentence Peggy winked in Tony's direction
"I think I can see what you're getting at, so what is it you're proposing?"
Peggy started to feel a bit more relaxed and to get comfortable she slipped off her coat. Originally she had envisaged being thrown out of the place with a flea in her ear but not now. Now she could see the man in front of her was listening and Peggy could also sense that he was more than a bit interested.
"Well this house is near to Petticoat lane and although I aint seen it yet I thought we could set up shop there. The plan is that I move in and take care of the girls, young ones mind! and you bring the

punters over every night. Not just the Tommy's on leave, I mean anyone who likes them young and believe me I've seen them lately and there's loads. We can charge extra for the girl's youth! Now don't go getting me wrong, I aint talking about babies here. I mean girls of say thirteen, fourteen or at a push even fifteen. As long as we can pass them off as younger then it don't really matter. If we go any younger than thirteen we risk Old Bill breathing down our necks and that aint no good for anyone."
Tony sagely nodded his head. Not one to have any real morals, the idea of the girl's ages didn't bother him. The woman sitting in front of him seemed as if she knew what she was talking about. On the whole it looked like a pretty good idea and pound signs began to register.

"So Peggy why exactly do you need me, what's to stop you just setting up on your own?"

"Well to be frank Mr Segretti, it aint worth the hassle. From time to time punters are going to turn nasty and that aint good for a young girl to see. I can't risk another firm trying to muscle in and there aint no one in the east end who don't fear you. Now unless I employ me own men I will need someone with a bit of clout to back me up, should the need arise of course. Besides all of that you're the one who has all the contacts."

"So just how do you plan on getting these girls to work for you? It's one thing to procure a twenty something who knows what she's getting into but teenagers can be tricky little fuckers and believe me I know! Also there's the problem of this girl you've met, how are you going to get her on board?"

"That Mr Segretti is my problem. I've been working the street long enough to know how to handle them. So then, are you interested?"

"Yes I am Peggy. I suggest when you've got things into place you come back and well talk some more, possibly get the wheels in motion. Now I don't want to come across rude but I am a very busy man."

"Yes of course you are and thank you for seeing me."

Peggy Spencer left the room and was almost bowing as she did so. Tony Segretti liked her cap in hand attitude and if things did progress, knew she would be a piece of cake to handle. Deep down Tony didn't think it would come to anything. In principle it was a good idea and if the old bird could pull it off then credit to her but for now he'd sit back and wait.

Peggy descended the stairs with a wide grin on her face and as she passed Stan the pot man, winked at him. Stan shook his head, he'd seen many things over the years and even though he didn't know what had passed between his boss and this woman, he had a bad feeling about it.

Out in the fresh morning air Peggy Spencer felt euphoric. True there was a lot of work to be done and getting Esther on side would be a challenge but

Peggy had always been up for that. Stopping at a small tobacconist she purchased a paper. News of the terrible atrocities that the Jews were experiencing had begun to break and the papers front covers were filled with images of marching Nazis. Peggy felt that once Esther read the stories she would be putty in anyone's hands. Peggy also knew that she had to tread carefully and for the time being at least would treat Esther with kid gloves.

As she walked through the streets she took a long hard look at her surroundings. The evacuations had started and many of the children, who had yet to be placed, were playing in the street with their gas masks draped across their chests. It never ceased to amaze her at how rapidly things were changing, oh there was still the great British mentality and stiff upper lip but people also seemed more sombre than in the past. The war didn't bother Peggy Spencer, after all she only had herself to take care of but for many who lived waiting for a telegram, life wasn't so rosie.

Soho was beginning to come alive and the young girls were starting to gather on the street. In her day it had been different, a Tom wouldn't venture out until evening and then it would have to be dark. Back then being a whore was a stigma that lasted the whole of a person's life. Most would do their best not to be branded but these girls were a new breed. They were suffering the hardship of war and viewed life as less valuable than their predecessors ever had. These women wanted cash and plenty of it and they didn't care how hard they had to work to get it. They were all well aware that a bomb could drop at any second and were just living life for the moment. Peggy Spencer liked their view on life, their less than moral work ethics but most of all she liked the idea of how rich the youngsters were going to make her.

CHAPTER FIFTEEN

After taking a leisurely walk back from her meeting with Tony Segretti, Peggy had mulled over in her mind all that they'd discussed. Thinking had always given her an appetite and today Peggy Spencer was ravenous. About to buy bacon at the shop below her home she'd thought better of it when she remembered Esther was Jewish. Opting for two pasties she climbed the stairs more than a little apprehensive. On the way back she'd tried to work out a strategy but none was forthcoming so instead she'd just decided, as far as Esther was concerned at least, to just go with the flow and see what happened.

The flat on Romilly Street ran horizontal to Old Compton. Still very much in the heart of Soho but not on the main thoroughfare which allowed Peggy a small amount of peace and quiet.

Her home was compact but Peggy Spencer had made it cosy. In fact it was the only place she had ever felt really safe. In the beginning she'd enjoyed the sex but as time moved on and she'd been manhandled more times than she cared to mention, the flat had become her only sanctuary. Decorated in a fashion not too dissimilar to Tony Segretti's office, it always seemed welcoming to Peggy and it was something she was proud of. Placing her key in the lock, she took a moment to compose herself.

Esther Goldman was seated at the small table in the living room when she walked in and as hard as she was, the older woman couldn't help but feel a little bit sorry for the girl. Esther's face was red and swollen from hours of crying and where last night she had appeared a young nubile woman, now in the cold light of day, Peggy could see that she was just a child.

A child who'd had her whole life torn apart in the space of a few hours.

"Hi there my pretty, how are you feeling today?"

Esther shrugged her shoulders and once more the tears began to flow.

Laying the paper onto the table Peggy walked into the kitchen and proceeded to heat the pasties. Placing the kettle onto the stove she sneaked a swift look into the living room and when she saw the girl had picked up the newspaper gently clasped her hands together. Ten minutes later she returned with two plates to find Esther Goldman engrossed in the tabloid.

"Here we are! This will put hairs on your bleeding chest and no mistake."

Peggy put the plates onto the table and gently stroked Esther's head.

"Dreadful aint it, the bastards want shooting for what they're doing to them poor Jews. Now then my lovely, as hard as it is we need to talk about your future."

"My future?"

"Esther my love, the country's in a right old state and there's no telling what them lot in government are going to do. Now the last thing we want is for you to be shipped off to god knows where and all because you aint got no one looking out for you."
Esther started to sob.
"Wooo wooo would they do that?"
"Aint no telling darling but I've been giving the matter some thought and I may have just come up with a solution."
Esther was now desperate and she gripped Peggy's hand as she spoke.
"Thank you, thank you so much."
"Well you aint heard what I got to say yet so don't go jumping the fucking gun!"
Esther Goldman was momentarily taken back. Hearing the woman swear like that was new to her and it shocked her to the core. Her facial expression didn't go unnoticed.
"Darling you're going to have to toughen up if you want to make it. Times are hard and only the strong will survive. Do you understand what I'm saying?"
Esther knew only too well and she eagerly nodded. In fact Esther Goldman would have done anything to get the woman on side and not be sent back to Germany.
"Right then! I've been speaking to a colleague of mine, well maybe he's a bit more than that; let's call him a business associate. Anyway Tony, that's his name by the way, Tony says you need a guardian.

All legal and proper like! If you get one of them then they can't send you away.
Peggy waited for a response and was already prepared to act surprised when the girl next spoke. "Would you be my guardian Peggy, oh please say you will."
Peggy breathed in deeply as if to let Esther know that this was a big deal and she would owe Peggy big time if she decided to help the girl.
"If it's what you want but well need to contact a solicitor. Tony said it could all be sorted in a couple of weeks, now are you sure that's what you want?"
"I am and thank you Peggy, thank you so much."
The next three weeks passed quickly and life for Esther Goldman was more settled. Peggy instructed a solicitor and told him she was as pure as the preverbal driven. As a spinster, she was living off a family inheritance and would swear to raise the girl as a good Christian. Due to the war and the fact that families were being bombed out left right and centre, no one challenged a woman who was willing to take in a young Jewish girl. It was something Peggy had hoped for and she wasn't about to be disappointed. On the day that she was made legal guardian things rapidly changed. Esther had seemed to come to terms with her loss and was looking forward to a bright future but when the official papers dropped onto the door mat, she instantly saw a different side to Peggy Spencer.
"Right! Get yourself dressed were going out."

"Where are we going Peggy?"

"Fuck me! Do you always have to ask so many bleeding questions? We're going to move into your house."

"Oh Peggy I don't think I could possibly live there again."

"I'm afraid you aint got much choice in the matter, not unless you want to go back to kraut land and take your bleeding chances."

There and then Esther Goldman knew she'd made a terrible mistake, a mistake she wouldn't be free of until she reached twenty-one. She could feel a lump form in her throat and she wanted to cry but instantly she pulled herself together. The Goldman's were made of stronger stuff and even if Esther had no control over her life, she wasn't about to let Peggy Spencer see how upset she was.

Turning from Wentworth Street into Bell Lane Peggy couldn't have been more pleased. The road was a fair size but with just one terrace of five large Victorian houses. The first was a second hand shop and Esther informed Peggy that Mr Abbott the owner only used the upper floors for storage as he lived over in Shoreditch. The next two had been converted into offices, which left the Goldman residence and one on the end that was now empty. The family who had occupied it had decided that it would be safer to see out the war somewhere in the Home Counties.

"So you lot aint very neighbourly round here then?"

Esther only glared in Peggy's direction.

The set up was perfect. Anyone coming or going in daylight hours would think that Peggy was a saint who took in waifs and strays. After dark when the daily occupants had gone home, then the lane would become her private little red light district.

Walking up to the front door Esther placed her key in the lock and sighed heavily. The house was deathly quiet as they entered. Breakfast crockery was still in the sink and a pungent smell of rotting food filled the air. Pushing open a window, Esther wrinkled up her nose.

"I forgot what a mess Id left the place in."

"Don't worry about that. Now role up your sleeves darling because there's work to be done."

By the end of the day the house had been cleaned from top to bottom, though it was more on Esther's part than Peggy's. Peggy Spencer was good at giving orders but when it came down to actual hard graft, she left that to others. Her mother had always told her she was a lazy little cow but Peggy preferred to call herself a leader. There were leaders and workers in this world and it was the leaders who survived, at least that's how Peggy Spencer saw it.

In the ensuing two weeks she had used up most of her life savings on decorating and purchasing furniture. It was a gamble but one that Peggy Spencer reckoned was worth a punt.

Tradesmen had been instructed to paint all of the

bedrooms in candy pink. Due to the war it had been difficult to obtain but Peggy was insistent that it must be this shade and nothing else. Soft furnishings were ordered from Harrods along with teddies and dolls for decoration. Peggy realised the importance of making the girls feel at home but also of psychologically reminding the punters that who they were having sex with were young, young and worth the exorbitant fee they were being charged. She felt it would give her the advantage to manipulate the men into behaving and realising how lucky they were. The opportunity, for want of a better phrase, to have sex with a child, wasn't that easily obtainable. Peggy knew that you could dress it up as much as you wanted but when it came down to brass tacks, a fourteen year old was still a child.

The ground floor reception room had been given an entirely different make over. The walls were scarlet red and large plush sofas were placed on all sides. Finally when it was all finished Peggy Spencer stood back and sighed but Esther was open mouthed with shock and horror.

"Oh my God! How could you do this to my home?"

Annoyed and upset that the girl didn't like her interior design, Peggy turned on Esther in anger.

"Shut the fuck up you little bitch! Just remember if it weren't for me you'd be in one of them camps by now and it's our home not yours. I'll tell you something for nothing girl, if you keep on back chatting me I'm going to relinquish me fucking guardianship! Then where would you be?" Esther had been following the newspapers on a daily basis and she knew only too well what was going on and the atrocities that her people were being put through. The threat of being sent to another country, worse still to one of the labour camps the papers kept on about, filled her with anxiety and dread, so she had no alternative but to go along with things. If Esther had been brighter and had more sense, she could have easily found out it was something that would never happen. Esther's naivety was a comfort to Peggy and she felt confident that she could continue without any more interference from the girl.

Due to the blitz and constant bombing in London, small orphanages had begun to spring up. They were only intended to be a temporary measure but with the war now raging across Europe it looked more likely that they would become permanent fixtures. One such place was situated on New Union Street in Finsbury Park. A disused store house had opened its doors to the damaged children of the city. Peggy Spencer had been hanging around the area for a couple of days now. She needed to pick the right girl and one who'd keep her mouth shut. That girl came in the form of Mabel Barker and she was exactly what Peggy had been hoping for. At ten precisely the children were ushered out side. It was play time for the younger kids and socialising for the older ones. A small wall ran along the side of the building and seated on top were all of the teenagers, mostly girls but there were a few boys. Peggy scanned them all and her eyes instantly stopped on one in particular. Small and petite she had a head of flaming red hair and a manner that told everyone around her she was in charge. Today her antics would have been considered bullying but back then and under the circumstances, she was someone to be looked up to by the others. Peggy witnessed the girl taking money from a few of the timid looking ones and she could see that hard cash meant a lot to Mabel. Her clothes were worn and tired but the girl had paid attention to her hair and Peggy could see the slight hint of rouge on her cheeks. Waiting patiently until she was able to corner Mabel alone, Peggy went in for the kill.

"Excuse me Miss but might I have a word?"

Mabel was suspicious and it was nothing to do with what she'd been through. Her background hadn't been good and by all accounts she was probably better looked after in the orphanage than she'd been by her family. As Mabel Barker was out to scam as many people as she could, she was suspicious that others were trying to do the same to her. With both hands on her hips and the corners of her mouth downturned, she cockily positioned her head so that her eyes stared up towards Peggy.

"What?"

"There's no need to be so bleeding rude young lady. I've got a proposition for you!"

Mabel instantly calmed down and after the pair introduced themselves the next hour was spent in the local cafe. The two had their heads bowed low and were deep in conversation for the entire time. Peggy explained to Mabel that she needed four girls and what she wanted them for. She also told Mabel that she would be well paid.

"So how much you offering Mrs?"

Peggy Spencer grinned. This young girl reminded her of herself so much. It was years ago now but she could clearly remember what it was like starting out on her own, trying every scam in the book just to earn a few bob.

"A pound a girl, then ten bob a week as a retainer."
"Wos a retainer?"

"It's a payment to keep you on board. Say one of the girls wants to leave, then you're back on the scene to get me another. Now there's a few conditions."

"Here we go! I thought there'd be a fucking catch."
"Oi watch your mouth! There aint no catch as you put it, just a few conditions. One, this must remain a secret as it aint exactly legal. Two, I don't want the girls to be under fourteen but I want them to look as though they are and three, any girl who joins us must do so freely and without pressure from you. The last thing we need is for some young brass to go running to the bleeding Old Bill. So

what do you say?"
"I say yes please Mrs! You're like a fucking modern day Fagin only instead of going out to rob, your little crew of girls are going to do it from the comfort of a nice warm house."
Peggy Spencer again wanted to chastise Mabel for swearing but at the same time she couldn't help but laugh. This girl was funny but above all she was street wise and it was something Peggy had hoped, no, needed to see. It was agreed that the two would meet up again in a week's time to see how things were progressing. After she watched Mabel disappear into the orphanage Peggy once again made her way over to Soho.
Tony Segretti was surprised to say the least when the woman entered his office. Initially he'd thought the idea was good but when three weeks had passed he hadn't expected to see Peggy again.
"Well this is a fucking turn up for the books and no mistake."
Peggy didn't see the relevance to what he was saying. Had he not thought she was serious with her plan? Tony Segretti had a lot to learn about the woman standing before him and it would take a while but he would eventually find out that there was a lot more to Peggy Spencer than he could ever have imagined.

CHAPTER SIXTEEN

Dulcie had been in Kirkby for a little over three months. The routine that the Dobson's had set her was backbreaking. Woken at five each morning she was expected to feed the chickens, collect the eggs then help Phyllis Dobson to prepare the breakfast. Each day her hosts would sit down to a full English and it always smelled and looked amazing. Unfortunately that was as far as it went for Dulcie; she was given a slice of bread and a spoonful of homemade jam. Only once had she asked why she didn't eat like Mr Dobson and her question was answered with a swift slap around the face from Phyllis.

"The lord doesn't like greedy children and I can see we have a lot of work to do with you Dulcie Gray!" After breakfast was finished Dulcie was sent into the field with Bert. He seldom spoke to her except to tell her when she wasn't working hard enough. Picking potatoes from the field along with hired locals brought little relief. Very few wanted to chat and most eyed the girl from London with suspicion but Dulcie couldn't understand the way they talked so she didn't mind that much. When she'd first arrived at the farm Dulcie had been a chubby girl of average height. Her mother had always told her that she'd been at the back of the queue when the looks were being dished out but it wasn't something that had ever worried her.

She soon gave up any hope of happiness and the way she was being treated began to show as the weight fell from her body. No one bothered and on the couple of days a week when she was allowed to attend the local school, the meagre lunch rations did nothing to help her gain weight. Dulcie's birthday came and went but there were no celebrations or presents, not even a card from her own mother. It was a sad fact but Rita Gray hadn't given her only child a second thought since the day she had been taken.

Bert Dobson was a weird introvert type and where at first Dulcie had thought he was the boss of the house, it soon became apparent that it was Phyllis who ruled the roost. Bert worked hard all day but his only reward was a hot meal. There were no kind words from his wife, only the constant referrals to the bible whenever she spoke. Dulcie was made to go to Sunday school each week. The tiny church hall was crammed with local kids who all took their religious studies very seriously. Dulcie Gray found it difficult as back in London she'd never had to endure Sunday school or get to grips with the bible. Many of her old class mates had been forced to endure it but not Dulcie, she would sit on the swings and wait until her pals were released, from what Dulcie liked to call Sunday bashing. Rita Gray had been a lot of things but god fearing wasn't one of them.

Now every Sunday when she returned from her class to the farm, Dulcie would have to recite all that had been taught and heaven help her if she got anything wrong. After the Dobson's devoured a large roast dinner and Dulcie had eaten the one slice of meat and a few vegetables that had been grudgingly put on her plate, she then spent the next hour scrubbing all the pots and pans. For the rest of the day until she was sent back to the barn it was constant prayer recital with Phyllis. With her eyes closed Dulcie would often drift off into a fantasy world other times she would silently call Phyllis Old bitch or just keep repeating in her head Fuck off fuck off fuck off.

In the last couple of weeks her body had started to feel funny and her tiny breasts had begun to hurt. There was no one to tell her about puberty and Dulcie just put it down to all the hard work she'd been doing. When she woke one morning to find blood on her nightdress she panicked. Without dressing Dulcie ran over to the farmhouse screaming. When she entered, Phyllis was standing at the sink but there was no concern for the girl, instead her voice rose to a thunderous crescendo.

"How dare you come into my home howling like a banshee?"

Dulcie turned and pulled at her nightdress to show the blood stain but Phyllis only shook her head in a show of disgust. Making her way over to the dresser she removed a few old rags and thrust them in Dulcie's direction. A couple fell to the ground and as Dulcie in her bare feet knelt down to pick them up she glanced upwards in Phyllis's direction. Her tearful eyes brought no mercy and Phyllis's face became even harder.

"That's the sigh of the devil girl; I always knew you were no good. It won't be long before the lads start sniffing around, and then folk will see just what a bad lot you are. Boys will try and take you into alleyways and force themselves on you. Their breath will be hot and they will slaver like dogs after a bitch on heat. I always told Bert it would be a mistake taking you in; London folk haven't any Christian morals. Now get back to the barn and clean yourself up."

Dulcie was scared but did as she was told through fear of getting another beating. When the same scenario occurred the following month she just got on with it. Washing the rags and hanging them out to dry became second nature and when she overheard other girls at school refer to their monthlies, she felt comforted in the realisation that she wasn't the only one. Around the same time that Dulcie started her periods, Bert Dobson had begun to act differently around her. A simple task like doing the dishes became embarrassing as his eyes followed her every move. The first time she really noticed there was a problem was one night after she'd finished her chores and had returned to the barn. With only the dull light from her small

lantern, Dulcie had just started on the first page of her favourite book when she heard shouting from the farm house. Quietly she crept across the yard and peered into the kitchen window. Phyllis was reading her husband the riot act and Dulcie could see that he had a pair of her knickers in his hand. All the while Phyllis ranted her husband continued to finger the cotton gusset of Dulcie's underwear.
"You disgust me Bert Dobson, you're nothing more than an animal and the Lord will strike you down for your evil thoughts."
"Maybe he will Phyllis but at least I will go a happy man."
Dulcie didn't like what she was hearing and decided to try and stay in the background in future. Quietly she made her way back to the barn and hid her head under the blanket. Inwardly Phyllis Dobson was enraged with jealousy. Not that she wanted her husband physically, that idea repulsed her. No it was the fact that since the little London whore had arrived he was now open with his lust and Phyllis felt threatened. As far as she was concerned it was all the fault of Dulcie Gray, before she'd arrived the couple had been fine. Bert's disgusting acts and fantasies were never mentioned but Phyllis instead punished the girl for the smallest mistake she made. The slaps turned into more severe beatings and the human hand was replaced with Bert's leather belt that hung on the back of the kitchen door. Dulcie only tried to fight back once and then she'd actually

managed to swing a punch at Phyllis. She soon wished she hadn't as she was knocked onto the hard flagstone floor and repeatedly kicked. Bert Dobson was present but instead of going to her defence he simply shook out his newspaper and carried on reading.

One cold night as Dulcie huddled in her bed shivering she heard the latch on her door creak. Grabbing the lantern she desperately tried to light it but her hands were shaking so much that she dropped the match box and the contents spilled onto the floor. Dulcie didn't need to see his face she instantly recognised the smell of Bert Dobson and when he knocked the lantern from her hand she gasped. The room was almost in darkness except for the eerie light of the moon that shone through the cracks and knot holes in the barn walls.

"What's the matter Mr Dobson?"

Dulcie tried to hide the fear that was evident in her voice but each word still quavered. He didn't answer her question and instead handed her a small tube of bright red lipstick.

"Put that on!"

As Dulcie wound up the red tip she gasped in horror. It was the same shade her mother wore and images of Rita and Arty invaded her mind.

"I won't!"

"Girl you'll do as you are told or receive a good thrashing."

Reluctantly and without a mirror Dulcie did as she

was ordered. Her eyes never left Burt Dobson's until he began to open the fly of his trousers and exposed a hard purple penis. He moved towards her and when his hips were level with Dulcie's face he spoke.

"Suck it!"

Dulcie started to cry but moving forward she did as she was told and took Burt's penis into her mouth. For an instant the idea of biting down hard crossed her mind but she knew it would only result in a beating. Slowly she began to suck and the taste was so salty that Dulcie fought hard to stop herself from gagging. Her ordeal was over in seconds as Burt Dobson was so excited that he ejaculated almost immediately. Buttoning up his trousers he didn't utter another word and as he closed the barn door Dulcie spat out the disgusting liquid in her mouth. Walking over to the water jug she gulped down mouthful after mouthful of water desperately trying to get rid of the taste.

All was normal for the next week but on Sunday evening the same scenario arose. This time Dulcie didn't have to be told and carried out the act without a word being spoken by her or Bert Dobson. Dulcie hated what she was being made to do but she also realised it could be a lot worse. In her naivety she thought this was as far as things would go. How wrong she was.

The following Sunday, for some strange reason it was always on a Sunday, Bert again walked into the

barn. Waiting for the lipstick to be handed to her Dulcie was shocked when Burt didn't give it to her. Relief washed over her and she thought that maybe it wasn't going to happen again, that was until she saw him once again open his trousers.
"It time you were broken in girl!"
"Oh please Mr Dobson, please don't hurt me."
Dulcie Gray began to cry but her tears were completely ignored.
Bert, still dressed in his trousers and a vest, slipped his arms from his braces and pushed Dulcie onto the bed.
"This will only hurt if you struggle now lift up that nightdress and spread your legs."
Climbing on top of her he proceeded to enter her and as Dulcie screamed out in agony Bert Dobson slammed his hand over her mouth. His body felt like a ton weight on her small frame and as he grunted and groaned Dulcie thought back to what Phyllis had said Their breath will be hot and they'll slaver like dogs after a bitch on heat. With all her might Dulcie tried to push him off but it was futile. A few minutes later he let out one long groan and ejaculated. Trying to kiss her, his huge mouth seemed to cover her face and Dulcie again struggled to push him off. This time she succeeded and jumping from the bed she shrank into the corner and sobbed. Bert Dobson stood up, buttoned his flies and pulled up his braces. He didn't apologise or tell her not to say a word. Bert wasn't scared; it

wasn't as if anyone would believe the little Londoner anyway. The oral sex had been just a taster and as he hadn't had sex with his wife for more years than he cared to recall, he was looking forward to a repeat performance the following week.

"Clean yourself up you little whore!"

Dulcie could only nod her head. Her whole body ached and she stayed in the corner for what seemed like an age but in fact wasn't much more than an hour. At last she made a decision. Packing her little suitcase she dressed as quickly as she could then opened the barn door. It was nearly seven thirty and she could see the lamp burning in the farmhouse window. The Dobson's were normally in their beds by eight so she waited by the door until the lamp went out. As quietly as she could Dulcie lifted the latch and crept inside. With only her lantern as light she made her way over to the dresser. Many times she'd seen Phyllis go to a particular draw where she kept her money to pay the butcher and baker. Luckily the housekeeping had only been topped up the day before and as Dulcie pulled open the drawer five one pound notes came into view. Once more she carefully opened the door and made her way into the cold night air. As long as Bert Dobson didn't return for second helpings, then Dulcie knew she had until the morning before she'd be missed.

It took her about forty five minutes to walk to

Kirkby train station and the weather had taken a turn for the worse. As her destination came into view Dulcie Gray looked a poor sight. She was soaked through to her skin and her hair was plastered to her face but she didn't care. The only thing she did care about was getting seen and being sent back to the Dobson's. It would be fifteen minutes until the nine o'clock pulled into the station and Dulcie hid in a disused engine shed until she heard her train approach. Not until the train had pulled out and she was on her way did Dulcie at last let out a sigh of relief.

Hours later when the smell of good old London town filled her nostrils Dulcie Gray cried out in happiness. She had never been so pleased to be home in all her life. Even in the early hours of the morning the place was alive and even though there were all manner of dangers, strangely she felt save. There was something about the smoke that to Dulcie was warm and cosy as if two big arms had wrapped themselves around her. Her ordeal of a few hours ago, though not forgotten, seemed to pale into insignificance now that she was on her home turf. Heading towards Shepherds Bush it was now almost three o'clock and the drunks and winos were still milling around. When she saw the men swaying in her direction Dulcie would hide in a shop doorway or quicken her pace. Playing over in her mind all that had happened Dulcie made a promise to herself. She would say sorry to her

Mother and beg for her forgiveness. If Rita wanted to entertain the whole bleeding army then it was alright with Dulcie, anything would be alright as long as she didn't get sent back to that godforsaken place. Finally she made it to her road but was instantly glued to the spot as she viewed the carnage that had once been Evesham Street. Smoke filled the air and Dulcie could smell a strange aroma that she couldn't recognise, she would later learn that it was the smell of burning flesh. Only a few houses remained standing as the majority had been reduced to a pile of rubble. Tears streamed down her face and a feeling of pain began to set in. Desperate to find her mother Dulcie pulled at the rubble brick by brick but it was futile. Glancing round for help she suddenly spied a familiar figure. The man stood with a look of total bewilderment on his face and as Dulcie slowly walked over to him he didn't acknowledge her.

"Mr Pullman!"

The man just stared at her for what seemed to Dulcie like an age. His eyes were glass like and dirt covered his cheeks.

"I don't believe it, why its little Dulcie Gray."

"Mr Pullman where's me mum?"

Horace Pullman started to cry and Dulcie placed her hand tenderly on the man's arm.

"She didn't make it love. The fucking Gerry's got her, my Gertie as well, most of the fucking street as it happens."

"When?"
"A few hours ago but thank the lord you're safe. Most of them who survived are down the Salvation Army, you should get yourself over there."
Horace Pullmans words fell on deaf ears as Dulcie was already half way down the street or what was left of it. She had dropped her suitcase but she didn't care. Dulcie ran and ran until she could hardly breathe, her heart was beating ten to the dozen and all she could think about was getting as far away as she could. In fact Dulcie ran and then walked for hours until she didn't have a clue where she was.

Esther Goldman had been sent out to fetch the morning papers. It wasn't that Peggy wanted to read them, more the fact that she wanted it reiterated to Esther just how lucky she was. The daily's were full of news on the Jews plight and although it made her feel physically sick, Esther Goldman couldn't stop herself from reading. Sitting on a bench at the end of Wentworth Street Esther momentarily raised her head from the broadsheet and noticed Dulcie slumped on the opposite side of the street. Curled into a tight ball Dulcie had managed to get a couple of hours sleep before the market traders had begun to set up. Rubbing wearily at her eyes she spotted Esther at the same time. Esther Goldman crossed the street and bending down offered Dulcie a hand to stand up.
"My you look the worse for wear, are you alright?"

The kind words instantly made Dulcie cry and tears spilled down her cheeks.

"Nnnnn no I'm not. Me house got bombed out and me mum with it, now I aint got a clue what to do!"

Esther felt great empathy for the young woman standing before her. Approximately the same age Esther knew just what her new acquaintance was feeling.

"The exact same thing happened to me, well not the house part but my mother and father were killed in a bombing. I live just around the corner and you're welcome to stay with me for as long as you like. I have to warn you my home isn't as traditional as it should be but then you'll learn all about that for yourself in due course. For now you need a good bath and a hot meal and that I can offer you in abundance."

Dulcie Gray embraced Esther and there and then a friendship formed. It would be an unbreakable bond that would last for the rest of their lives.

CHAPTER SEVENTEEN

When Esther and Dulcie walked into the house on Bell Lane all hell was breaking loose. Peggy stood in the lounge with four young girls in front of her and she was almost shrieking as she spoke.
"I aint fucking having it do you hear me. I aint working me bleeding arse off for you lot to lie about and not do what you're fucking paid for."
Mabel Barker had done her job well and the girls she'd procured, Dottie Clarke, Blanche Andrews, Lilly Hawkins and Rose Smith looked no more than about twelve years old. In reality they were all over fourteen and by all accounts were now young women. Peggy had been delighted and by the time she had braided their hair and chosen pretty dresses, they now appeared the epitome of innocence.
Peggy finally stopped ranting and told the girls to go to their rooms and give them a good clean.
"Not you Lilly Hawkins, I want a fucking word with you. It's come to my attention that you're giving away fucking services for free!"
"I aint Peg, honest I aint."
"Don't fucking lie to me because you was seen last night giving that young soldier a blow job. He paid for straight sex and nothing else. Lilly you might be a horny little bitch and that aint none of my concern but bleeding hell girl charge for it! Carry on like

this and well all be broke and out on the street before too long. And just what is that bottle of peroxide doing in the bathroom?"
"I'm going to dye me hair and look like Mae West!" The look of shock and horror on Peggy's face was plain for all to see.
"You will do no such bleeding thing Lilly Hawkins. I'm warning you, if you change the way you look then you'll be out of this house as fast as I can fucking throw you. Understood?"
"But Peggy...."
Esther rolled her eyes and beckoned for Dulcie to follow her. Climbing two flights of stairs they at last arrived at Esther's attic room. Dulcie was surprised, the room was spacious and decorated in the height of fashionable taste. The one thing that did trouble her was the large bolt on the back of the door. She didn't want to pry but even after this short space of time things were starting to play on her mind.
"Esther please don't take this the wrong way and don't think I'm ungrateful but this is a fucking weird set up if you don't mind me saying. I'm happy to be here but what the bleeding hell was going on down there?"
"My dear friend, my only friend you wouldn't believe it if I spent the next hour telling you."
"Well neither of us have got anything else to do so you might as well give me the gen so to speak. I think I've got a bit of an idea, I aint as green as I'm

cabbage looking you know."
Esther Goldman did as she was asked and spent the following hour relaying all that had happened to her. When she at last finished and turned to her new friend, Dulcie sat opened mouthed.
"Told you it was unbelievable."
"Listen, with what I've been through recently nothings unbelievable!"
Esther looked bewildered so Dulcie in return relayed all that had happened to her. She started with her father's death, then the evacuation and didn't stop till she had reached her home town again.
"So that man raped you?"
"Call it what you will but it weren't fucking pleasant I can tell you."
Both young girls started to laugh and fell back onto the bed in a fit of giggles. They only stopped when Peggy's voice was heard booming up the stairs.
"Esther Goldman get your scrawny fucking arse down here this instant!"
"Oh god it's the wicked witch herself, best do as she wants. Come on Ill introduce you. This is going to be interesting."
The two descended the stairs but as they reached the bottom Esther stopped and grabbed Dulcie's arm.
"No matter what she says just ignore it."
"What do you mean?"
Esther smiled.

"She can be a right cow sometimes but I've come to learn that her bark is worse than her bite. If she's rude to you ignore her and if she's overly nice just be careful."

By the time they reached the living room Lilly had long retreated to her room in shame. Peggy Spencer now stood alone in the lounge and with her hands on her hips she didn't look happy. With a fake smile, the friendliest she could offer under the circumstances, she then introduced herself. Things were looking up and this little waif had a cuteness about her. Esther Goldman introduced Dulcie Gray but when she got to the part where Dulcie would be staying with them Peggy's mood instantly changed.

"That aint going to fucking happen young lady! And besides were full to bursting with the other girls. Now bid your friend goodbye as there's plenty of chores need doing."

Peggy was about to leave the room when she was momentarily stunned by Esther's words. The girls voice rose and she spoke with such authority that Peggy started to worry.

"Yooooou! will not tell me who I can and cannot invite into my home Peggy Spencer! I may have been gullible when it came to letting you be my guardian. I may have kept quiet when you turned my house into a common brothel but you do not have cart blanch to tell me who can be my friend. I will have here whoever I please, no matter what you say. Furthermore Dulcie will not be one of

your tarts, she's my friend and a guest."
With that Esther turned and stormed up the stairs with Dulcie Gray following in hot pursuit. They could both hear Peggy ranting Well she can bleeding work for her keep then and Esther immediately knew this was one battle she had won. Peggy Spencer was in a slight panic. The girl was growing up fast and time was moving quickly. If she didn't give Esther a bit of slack now and again then she could for all intent and purpose go to the authorities. It would only take a word of advice from someone and she could have them all out on their arses.

Dulcie Gray settled in very quickly. She shared a room with Esther and carried out chores to cover the cost of her food. Peggy at times could be a task master but nothing compared to how the Dobson's had treated her. Her nights were spent peacefully and with the aid of the lock on her door she didn't have to worry about any unwelcome visitors. Most of the girls in the house were friendly, though Dulcie did try and distance herself from them. She didn't view herself as better but still the things they got up to in their rooms each night disgusted her. There were many times as she and Esther lay in bed they could hear all manner of sounds from the rooms below. Dulcie didn't mind the giggles and groaning and sometimes it even made her and Esther laugh out loud. It was the odd occasions when one of the girls could be heard crying, that was the sound she didn't like as it reminded her of Bert Dobson and what he had done to her.

Peggy Spencer soon formed a different opinion of Dulcie and had, though she wouldn't admit it to anyone, grown rather fond of the girl. She worked hard, unlike Esther, who refused to lift a finger. Peggy supposed when all was said and done it was to be expected, after all Esther had been well and truly duped.

When Dulcie Gray had been resident at Bell Lane for a little over three months things suddenly changed. Peggy had been busy of late, each night Tony Segretti was bringing more and more soldiers over so she hadn't spent much time with the youngsters who resided in the upper room. On the whole Tommy's were a randy lot but not that clean. Twice in the last month she'd had to take Dottie to the quack as she'd caught a dose and what a palaver that had been. Instead of the girl looking childlike Peggy had reversed things so as not to arouse suspicion and dressed her as grown up as she could. Luckily the doctor was used to the scenario and didn't make a comment but Tony was going to have to be a bit more choosey.

Dulcie was in the lounge on her hands and knees cleaning out the grate as Peggy entered.

"Morning Dulcie love, now where did I put that...... Fucking hell!"

Dulcie had stood up to take a breather and a clear bulge was visible in the front of her dress.

"Tell me you're not up the bleeding duff girl!" Dulcie Gray gave a slight grin and shrugged her shoulders. It had only dawned on her a couple of weeks before when her period hadn't appeared for the second time and she'd started to feel sick. Confiding in only Esther, the two had decided to keep it a secret for as long as possible but now her dresses had begun to pull at the seams there wasn't a lot she could do to hide it. Peggy's reaction surprised Dulcie; all the woman did was sigh heavily and shake her head.

"It's going to be a lot of extra bleeding work you know. Are you ready for that? because none of us can carry you love. You know as well as I do that we all have to pull our weight round here."

"There aint a lot I can do about it now, is there?"

"There's always something you can do darling. I know an old girl a few streets away that will get rid, if that's what you want?"

Dulcie Gray was horrified. True it had been a shock when she'd realised what was happening but getting rid had never entered her head.

"Never! Look I aint got no family to call me own anymore so me and Esther's decided we are going to raise it and care for it."

"On your head be it but don't say I didn't bleeding warn you."

Six months later and in the middle of a busy night of punters everyone in the house heard Dulcie Gray scream out in pain. Peggy flew up the stairs and

when she entered the girls room saw Esther mopping her friends brow with a wet flannel.
"Fuck me this is all I need, come on out of the bleeding way! Esther get down these stairs and tell those little bitches to get back to work, then bring a bowl of hot water and some towels. Well go on then, what are you waiting for?"
Peggy Spencer rolled up her sleeves and smiled down at a dishevelled Dulcie who was groaning on the bed in agony.
"This is nothing love, when it really starts its going to hurt like no pain you've ever felt before or will again, it'll put you off men for life I can tell you."
The pain was making Dulcie ratty and she hissed out her words between contractions.
"How urghhhh the fuck would urghhhh you know? You aint never even had a kid!"
 "My Darling girl there's a lot you don't know about me. When I first went on the game I was as naive as a baby and within six months was up the duff. I couldn't work and had no one to take care of me, what choice did I have? The old bitch that got rid was a dirty cow and when the kid was out of me I got an infection. Quack said I'd never have another one but there you go, that's life. There's been times when I would have given me back teeth to go through what you are now but it wasn't to be and in my line of work probably weren't a bad thing."
"Urghhhhhh."
"That's it love you bear down, where the fucks

Esther with them towels?"

Just as she spoke Esther Goldman returned. All was now quiet downstairs and Peggy turned her attention to the task in hand. Rolling up one of the small towels she handed it to Dulcie.

"Every time the pain comes, bite down on this. I know it aint nice but fuck me girl you aint half making a din. Last thing we need is to scare off all me fucking punters."

For the first time the three women all laughed together and Esther saw Peggy Spencer in a slightly better light. It was another ten hours before Dulcie's baby was born but when she clapped eyes on her for the first time, Dulcie Gray instantly fell in love. Esther was jumping for joy and even Peggy, as hardnosed as she was, had tears in her eyes.

"Oh what a little beauty! What are you going to call her."

Dulcie Gray looked down at the tiny bundle; her hair was as black as night and she had the prettiest rose bud mouth.

"Olivia, Olivia Esther Gray and I'm going to call her Livy for short."

Esther Goldman beamed from ear to ear. She had no idea that her friend would include her name and Esther was as proud as punch.

As each of the girls finished their shift for the night they one by one came to welcome the new arrival to Bell lane. Cooing and billing they kissed Olivia's tiny head but when they held the baby for too long

Esther would gently lift her up and place her back into Dulcie's arms. It was a comical scene, almost as if Esther had taken on the role of the doting farther. In some ways that's exactly what she'd done and in the ensuing months she would equally share child care with her best friend. Olivia Gray was a dream baby and never cried but then she was never short of attention. Peggy and the other girls in the house adored her and the baby soon had several surrogate mothers. Nights were a struggle as they tried to keep the place quiet after settling Livy down. It wasn't easy as the punters were often drunk and would be singing at the top of their voices. One such evening saw Olivia screaming in fear after Dottie Clarke began to shriek out in the room below. Peggy was first on the scene and she didn't knock before entering Dottie's room.

"For fucks sake girl whatever's all the bleeding noise about."

"I'm sorry Peg but this dirty bastard aint clean."

Peggy Spencer eyed the soldier suspiciously.

"What are you on about Dottie?"

"Well he wanted a blow job but his cocks all crusty."

"Crusty!"

"Yeah and there's stuff coming out of it. I aint putting that in my mouth for no amount of bleeding money."

Peggy didn't need any further information and instantly told the man to leave and not come back. Esther had been looking over the top banister as he left and she sighed deeply. This couldn't continue. Livy had to be brought up in a calm homely environment. Then and there Esther decided that one way or another the brothel must close. Wanting something and making it happen were two different matters and quite how she would achieve this, was at the moment beyond her.

CHAPTER EIGHTEEN
January 1945

The war was slowly coming to an end and the Yanks were well ensconced on English soil. Most were stationed in the Home Counties but when they had leave would venture to the smoke for some well earned fun. Things couldn't have been better for Tony Segretti; he loved the Americans and all the money that they had to spend. Recently he'd begun to break the rules Peggy had set regarding who he took to Bell Lane. She didn't mind soldiers though she would have preferred them to have been officers but Peggy couldn't afford to be too choosey. At the end of the day it was the cash that was the most important thing. Originally Peggy had wanted the place to be up market and special, after all, what she was offering was special. It might have been an acquired taste but young kids weren't readily available in Soho. That would rapidly change in the future but for now Peggy ruled her little empire like a queen. The girls had been replaced eighteen months earlier when they had started to look older. Lily and Rose had moved to one of Tony's places and were now well established as exceptional whores. Learning their game at an early age had made them both experts in the sex trade. Dottie had married one of her clients and moved to Texas never to be heard from again and Blanche landed a job at Harrods on haberdashery as a counter girl. When Esther and Dulcie went shopping they would often pop in to see her but as the months went on it was clearly visible that their visits weren't welcome.

It had taken a while for Peggy to replace them all as Mabel Barker was doing a five stretch in Holloway for blackmail. It hadn't surprised Peggy, the girl was rotten through and through. That much had been evident when she'd coerced her own friends into becoming prostitutes and had taken money for it too.

The new girls were street wise and from the off had demanded more money. Peggy knew she had little choice but to pay them what they wanted. Like the original crew these girls were all over fourteen but looked about twelve. In fact Peggy had given herself a pat on the back as they were more childlike than the girls Mabel had supplied. Cynthia, Bella, Annie and Frieda quickly settled in and it was soon business as usual.

Dulcie normally got on well with all the girls but there was something about Cynthia she couldn't take too. The girl was friendly enough but she seemed sneaky and to Dulcie a little weird. Several times, Dulcie had tried to tell Peggy that this one was bad but Peggy had always dismissed her and had even once accused her of being jealous. In the end Dulcie had given up trying but she still watched Cynthia like a hawk.

On New Year's Eve Tony Segretti had turned up at

Bell Lane with a van full of soldiers, far more than Peggy was happy with. They were all well on their way to being drunk and looked shabby and dirty. She felt Tony was abusing the girls and was taking advantage of her. It wasn't just the fact that he helped himself to the girls free of charge whenever he wanted but also that he seemed to look on them not as human beings but as animals to be used as he pleased. The men who accompanied him tonight entered the house in a rowdy manner. Peggy Spencer did her best to be polite but as they roughly manhandled the girls her patience wore thin. Grabbing Tony's arm, himself well oiled she led him into the kitchen.

"What the fuck are you playing at?"

"Come on Peggy love don't be like that, the boys only want a shag."

"Want a shag! Do you realise it'll take the girls all night to get through that lot? and look at the state of them!"

"Yeh but think of the reddies well earn and I've got another load coming over later."

Peggy was about to continue her argument when an almighty scream ran out. Rushing from the kitchen she scanned her eyes in all directions. Cynthia Fox, the newest recruit of the four, mouthed the name Frieda then pointed towards the ceiling. Peggy charged up the stairs and bursting through the bedroom door found Frieda hunched on the floor. Blood was streaming down her face where she'd been punched and large purple welts had already begun to form on the top of her arms.

"What the fucks going on here?"

A thick set American, partially dressed in his uniform, the top half only, was struggling to pull on his trousers as he began to drawl on in an accent that Peggy had come to loath.

"I paid good money for that little bitch and now she won't do what I want. You London whores are all the same!"

"Now just you hold on a minute me old china! Frieda what's wrong?"

With tears streaming down her face Frieda Wallace wiped the back of her hand across her nose and a long candle of snot smeared over her cheek.

"Peg I'm usually up for anything you know that but this dirty bastard tried to push his cock up me arse. I aint doing that no matter how much he's fucking paying do you hear me."

If Peggy was anything she was fair and she never forced her girls to do anything they didn't feel happy with. Turning on the American her words came out with a vengeance and the soldier wiped his face as her spittle showered him.

"You dirty cunt! In all my years on the game I never let anyone take me up the fucking rear. I suggest you fuck off out of here and bleeding well don't come back."

"I paid fare and square and if I don't get my money's worth I'm going to call on the police."

"I'd like to see you fucking try old mate! Just how are you going to explain what you was doing here with a kid in the first place. You thick fucking Yank!"

Suddenly it dawned on the soldier that his platoon officer would be informed and he turned from the room. As he descended the stairs he could be heard cursing all the English whores to hell and back.

Peggy knelt down beside Frieda and took her in her arms.

"Did he hurt you love?"

"Not too bad but I think me arse hole is going to be sore for a few days."

Peggy couldn't help but laugh and the sound of her laughter brought a small giggle from Frieda's mouth.

The volume of men Tony Segretti was bringing to the Bell Lane house continued and soon took its toll. Peggy had noticed that a couple of the girls were looking overly tired. Bella in particular was beginning to get dark circles under her eyes. To stop the further decay of her girls looks, Peggy stated that from now on all Mondays would be a day of rest. It was to be a woman only zone and the only day that Peggy wouldn't allow a man in the house. All the girls had been looking so tired lately and they all needed at least one day off a week. Dulcie always cooked them a big roast dinner with all the trimmings and the afternoon would be spent playing games with Olivia. For one day a week the young women, who had so quickly hardened to the life they now led, were once more children themselves. Peggy would watch them all in turn and smile. Her life was good and the nest egg she had stashed away would see her alright in her old age.

It was a Friday night in March that things started to crumble and the seed was set for Peggy's little empire on Bell Lane to fall. It would take a few months but life as they all knew it would soon come to an end.

Tony Segretti had brought over three English service men and they were sitting in the lounge waiting for the girls to come down. Peggy had joined the men and was making idle chit chat when Cynthia entered the room. Seconds later Annie followed and it was clear to all that she'd been drinking. Peggy couldn't say anything but made a mental note to give her hell once their company had been serviced. Draping themselves over two of the men the girls soon began to pet heavily. Bella was ill in bed with a chest infection so it only left Frieda to make an appearance. Peggy gave a cough, an agreed signal; it was the girls cue to take their clients upstairs. Tony Segretti was sharing a scotch with the remaining soldier and he apologised for the man's wait, at the same time he gave Peggy a steely glare and it was obvious he wasn't happy. Needing to stop the soldier complaining about the wait, Tony continued chatting.

"I tell you what pal, you aint going to be disappointed with the girl she's real special. I had her myself a couple of weeks back and she's got the tightest juiciest little cunt ever. I mean this girl is a real professional, the things shell do to you is fucking mind blowing. She's got the peachiest little arse and suck? she can suck for bleeding England!" Now the soldier was getting excited, so excited Tony thought he was going to come there and then. "Would she lick me balls? I've always fancied that." "Lick your balls? Mate shell lick anything you fucking ask her to. I got her to start at me feet and work her way up, a real turn on that is. By the way she fucks like a rabbit, that's if you get that far, know what I mean? I can honestly say you're going to heaven with this little bitch."

Joe Wallace had been in France for the last eight months and on his first day home had decided to stay in London for a little light relief before joining his family. He wasn't aware that all but one of his family had been blown to bits a few weeks earlier. Even though the ARP wardens had tried to sift through the rubble there was no paperwork or details left so it was difficult to certify who had actually died. Joe was a proud dad and loved his son and daughter more than anything else in life. His boy was only ten but his young daughter was approaching fifteen and becoming a right handful, if her mother's letters were anything to go by. When the lounge door at last opened and Frieda flounced in dressed in a sheer negligee, Joe Wallace flew to his feet.

"What the fuck do you call this?"

Tony Segretti and Peggy both laughed and in unison said Lovely aint she.

"Fucking lovely? She's my daughter you dirty cunts!"

A split second later and Joe had dived onto Tony knocking him to the floor. Frieda was screaming and Peggy tried desperately to get Joe off of Tony. The soldier had managed to straddle Tony and was repeatedly punching him in the face. Tony Segretti tried to defend himself but the soldier was much bigger and stronger. Things seemed to happen in slow motion and Peggy Spencer clearly saw the soldier remove a handgun but could do nothing to stop it.

"Rot in fucking hell you cunt!"

A loud bang rang out and a second latter Tony Segretti lay contorted on the floor in agony. He held his hand to his stomach wound but blood pumped freely through his fingers. Frieda Wallace had gone into shock and just stared down at the carnage. After hearing the shot, one of Joe's comrades ran down into the hall. Peggy knew she had to take control and ordered the men, along with Frieda, to leave at once. Escorting them to the door she pulled a trench coat from the stand and passed it to Frieda. They were all ashen in colour but Peggy assured them that there would be no come

back and that it would all be hushed up. The Soldiers didn't need telling twice and Peggy was soon alone in the hall. Making her way upstairs she found Bella asleep and Annie passed out from the alcohol. At least not having to explain things to them was less of a burden on her. Cynthia was nowhere to be seen and Peggy guessed she'd gone off with her customer in the hope of earning a little private cash. It was becoming a habit and one Peggy would have to nip in the bud but for now she had more important things on her mind. Peggy glanced upwards and momentarily considered informing Dulcie and Esther but thought better of it. If they hadn't heard then all well and good but if they had then they weren't in a position to call the police, not if they wanted to keep a roof over their heads. Her little Toms had been her main concern and as two of them were both out for the count and the other one was AWOL she didn't have to worry. With a heavy heart she once again made her way back down to the lounge. The sight before her looked worse than a few moments ago. She wasn't much of a medic but by the loss of blood and the guts that had now begun to emerge from Tony Segretti's stomach, Peggy could tell he didn't have long.
Esther, having been woken by all the commotion, came downstairs and walked into the lounge to see what the noise was about. She almost fainted when she saw Tony covered in blood."Oh my god! I

knew something like this would happen one day."
"Bleeding hell Esther I do not need to hear I told you so now is Livy asleep?"
"Yes but....."
"Don't give me fucking buts, get up those stairs and tell Dulcie I need her help."
"What for?"
Frustrated, Peggy let out a large sigh.
"To throw a party! What the fuck do you think, bury him of course?"
"But Peggy you can't do that, the poor man's still breathing."
"Believe you me he won't be for much longer, now go!"
When Ester Goldman had left the room Peggy placed two fingers onto Tony's neck. His pulse was so faint she could barely feel it and pulling a cushion from the sofa she placed it over his face. Suddenly Tony's arms began to tear at the fabric and Peggy had to lean down on the cushion with all her weight. It was only a few seconds before Tony Segretti's resistance subsided; he had no more strength left in him. His life ebbed away and by the time Dulcie and Esther returned, Peggy had wrapped the body in a large sheet.
"Right you two, we need to get him down the cellar till the morning, Dulcie get his legs and Esther don't stand there fucking gawping open the bloody door."
It took a few minutes but the women finally

managed to place Tony's body in the basement and Peggy swiftly locked the door and placed the key on top of the dresser. Holding a hand to her chest Peggy Spencer was breathing hard and Esther and Dulcie both noticed that she appeared to be in pain.
"Are you all right Peg?"
"What you on about of course I bleeding am. Now we've got a lot of scrubbing to do before the morning. Esther! tomorrow when the girls get up, you can take them and Livy shopping ok. No one is to mention a word of this to the others. As far as they are concerned, Tony got injured but he's alright. Now come on the pair of you look lively and let's just hope we can get it done before bloody Cynthia comes home."
The three scrubbed and scrubbed and finally there was no trace of blood left in the room. They got to bed at around three o'clock but were all awake again by five. The image of a dead man with his guts spilling out had played heavily on the minds of Esther and Dulcie. Peggy wasn't as bothered but she just wanted to be sure that none of the others were poking their noses into things that didn't concern them.
Doing as she'd been asked Esther set out on a mammoth shopping trip. Peggy had provided some cash and told her not to return until after lunch. As soon as they were out of the house she instructed Dulcie to fetch a spade from the outside shed.

"What are we going to do with him Peg?"
"You know that little bit of grass behind the Anderson shelter where Esther always says she's going to plant veggies? Well it will be Tony resting in that soil instead of the veg!"
It took Peggy Spencer three hours to dig a hole. It wasn't the traditional six feet deep grave but it was near enough. When it came to getting Tony Segretti's body back up from the basement it took all the strength that the two could muster. The bed sheet was almost completely crimson and Dulcie grimaced as she helped Peggy haul him up the stairs. Pushing the corpse into its grave was relatively easy but Dulcie could see that the hole wasn't big enough.
"Oh Peggy! now what we going to do?"
"Get out of me way you light weight. Honestly the youth of today aint got no fucking go in them." Peggy Spencer almost fell into the hole as she huffed and puffed. Pulling and shoving she manoeuvred Tony's body into an unnatural position until he was at last packed into the makeshift grave.
"There we go! aint a bad job even if I do say so myself. There's only one spade so go get the coal scuttle and start filling him in."
Dulcie did as she was asked and a short time later they both wiped the dirt from their hands and surveyed their handy work.
"Well I hope the poor fucker rests in peace Dulcie girl. Now we just got to hope that fucking stray

don't come round and start digging him up."
Something about Peggy's words struck a comical cord with Dulcie and as ashamed as she felt, she couldn't for the life of her stop laughing.
"Aint bleeding funny girl, if we get caught for this well all bleeding swing."
Those solemn words instantly stopped Dulcie laughing and she knew that whatever happened she must never breathe a word of what had gone on, not to another living soul.

CHAPTER NINETEEN

The next few weeks passed with little upset but Dulcie and Peggy were constantly checking to make sure the grave hadn't been interfered with. Apart from one small incident all was well. It had happened on a Sunday morning. Dulcie was desperate for the loo but as usual Cynthia had taken up residence in the bathroom. Making her way to the outside lavatory Dulcie spied the stray moggy that Peggy had warned her about. The tatty looking cat was on top of the grave furiously digging. Panicking, Dulcie was just about to shoo it away when it turned and had a shit in the hole it had just dug. When it finished, it meticulously back filled the hole. Dulcie began to giggle and then clamped an arm around her own stomach desperate to copy the strays own movements of a second before. In a quiet whisper she spoke to herself Thank the lord we have a bog or I think I'd be shitting on poor old Tony as well, then Dulcie flew into the outside privy and burst into laughter.

Peggy was managing to run Bell Lane without Tony Segretti. Over the last couple of years she had made several contacts in the Soho pubs that were willing to send round customers, so his loss wasn't a major hit to the business. It wasn't as busy as before but now that they were one girl down, since Frieda's hasty departure, it suited them. Peggy had decided against replacing her as Cynthia, Bella and Annie were coping well with the soldiers who called. Peggy had noticed that the animosity between Dulcie and Cynthia Fox was growing. She heard them arguing one morning and stormed into the kitchen to find them going at it like hammer and tongs.

"What the fucks going on in here?"

They both spoke at once; trying to get their point across first but Peggy wasn't having any of it. The scenario was becoming all too frequent and to be quite honest Peggy Spencer was tired of it.

"You can both scream at me till you're bleeding blue in the face but I aint listening. Now calm down! Right Dulcie you first, what's the problem?"

"She reckons I aint pulling me weight Peg, says I'm a fucking leech!"

"Is that what you said?"

Cynthia fox narrowed her eyes. She didn't like Dulcie and when it came down to brass tacks she wasn't that keen on Esther either but accepted she had to be nice to her as it was Esther's house.

"Yeah I damn well did. I'm the one selling me bleeding arse every night while her and the other one upstairs have a life of fucking luxury." They are both older than me but I'm the one doing all the work. It just aint fair Peg."

Peggy was running out of patience. If it wasn't one thing it was another and she didn't know just how long she could carry on. Since Tony's death Peggy hadn't felt well and the last thing she wanted was to have to deal with two fighting young bitches who didn't know how lucky they were.

"Look! You knew the score when you came here Cynthia so why are you bleating about it now."

Cynthia Fox shrugged her shoulders and it annoyed Peggy even further.

"If you think you can fucking do better elsewhere then sling your bleeding hook because I've just about had a gut full. Dulcie you can take that smug grin off your face as well because you do little to keep the peace. Now for fucks sake give it a rest the pair of you."

With that Peggy Spencer marched out of the room, grabbing her coat and hat she left the house.

Cynthia and Dulcie just stared at each other, neither was prepared to back down but both were a little shocked at Peggy's reaction. Normally she would have moved heaven and earth to sort out a problem and keep everyone happy. Peggy wanted a peaceful house but today something was wrong, today she just couldn't be bothered.

Walking along Bell Lane she turned into Harrow Place and finally reaching her destination, Peggy rapped on the doctors door. A National Health Service was being talked about but had yet to come into force. Gratis treatment was available down at the Royal Free Hospital but that seemed like miles away and Peggy just wasn't up to travelling. Doctor Whissy had treated the local community for years and Peggy had even taken the girls to him when

they'd come down with a dose. Now that she was the one seeking treatment Peggy Spencer wasn't so confident.
The door was at last opened and on seeing who his caller was, the small man wearing round horn rimmed spectacles motioned with his hand for her to come in.
"Good morning Peggy and what can I do for you on this fine day."
As he spoke Doctor Whissy strained his neck trying to glance over her shoulder. Expecting to see one of the lovely young ladies that were usually with Peggy, he was disappointed when he realised she was alone.
"For once doctor Whissy it's about me. I really don't feel well and was wondering if you had a tonic or something to give me a bit of a pickup.
"All in good time Peggy but I need to carry out an examination first. Goodness me I've been seeing you in my surgery for a few years now but it's the first time you've ever asked for medical help for yourself."
"Good fucking constitution that's why, strong as a bleeding ox I am."
Bartholomew Whissy produced a stethoscope and over the next few minutes carried out a thorough examination of his patient.
"Peggy your heart seems to be missing a beat and I would like you to go into hospital for a few tests."
"Get away with you Doc, I aint got time for no

hospitals I've got a house to run."
Well aware what she meant, Dr Whissey held up his hand to stop Peggy talking. Her blood pressure was sky high and her heart was missing more than just the odd beat. He needed to instil in Peggy just how important a visit to the Royal Free was.
"Miss Spencer if you do not go then there is a grave danger that your house will soon be running itself. I cannot stress how important this is. Peggy I feel you may have degenerate heart disease, now do I make myself clear?"
"What the fucks degenerative heart disease?"
"It could be one of several things but what I do know is that it can lead to sudden death, now do you really want to take that chance?"
Peggy didn't reply and as Doctor Whissy made a telephone call informing the hospital of her arrival he could clearly see beads of sweat forming on her brow.
"Right then! I need to get home and pack a bag."
"Peggy there isn't time for that! Your case is so urgent that I'm taking you there and admitting you myself. Time really is of the essence here I'm afraid!"
The Royal Free hospital was situated in Hampstead and in nineteen forty five would take at least a half hour to reach. Bartholomew Whissey's old Ford screeched to a halt outside the hospitals main entrance and the car door flew open. Peggy was clutching her chest and the man knew that it was

vital he got her treatment immediately. Rushed into intensive care, Peggy Spencer's life hung by a thread. Bartholomew Whissey stayed for as long as he could but with patients to see, he asked the staff nurse to call when there was any news.

By nightfall and with no sign of their matriarch Dulcie and the girls were beginning to worry. Esther was hoping that Peggy wouldn't return though she didn't voice her opinion. Over the last couple of years she had come to like Peggy but she still wanted her house back and that, as far as she was concerned, couldn't come soon enough. Things were still strained between Dulcie and Cynthia but for Peggy's sake Dulcie had decided to make an effort. When the doorbell rang out Cynthia had already turned in for the night but Bella, Annie and Dulcie were in the lounge chatting. Going to the door, Dulcie wasn't surprised as she opened it to see a couple of soldiers on the step and called out You've got business! Showing the men into the lounge she instructed the girls to sort them out. Deciding to turn in she made her way upstairs and tapped on Cynthia's door as she passed. When there was no answer Dulcie just shrugged her shoulders and continued up the next flight of stairs to Esther.

Livy had been playing up which was unusual for her and Dulcie had told Esther that she needed a firm hand. Esther couldn't bring herself to chastise Livy so now every night for the last week bedtime

had turned into an ordeal. The child was so tiny but as headstrong and stubborn as a mule and Dulcie knew that came from her and not Burt Dobson.
"Olivia Gray get into that bleeding bed right now! Honestly Esther I don't know why you put up with the little cows shenanigans."
"Because my dear Dulcie I love the little mite no matter what mischief she gets up to."
Dulcie smiled at her friend. The three of them were like a little family and she didn't know how she would have survived if it hadn't been for Esther Goldman.
"Right Livy! Me and you need to have a little talk." Lifting the child onto the bed Dulcie sat down next to her.
"You can stop your bleeding high jinks this instant because if you don't there's not going to be a party next month.
Livy's mouth dropped at the corners, her eyes filled with tears and both of the women simultaneously got lumps in their throats. Olivia Grey had learnt very early on how to manipulate and at the drop of a hat she could now wrap them both round her little finger.
"I'm sorry mummy."
"That's alright then; well say no more about it. Now hop into bed and Aunty Esther will tuck you in and read you a story."
Olivia did as her mother asked and as Dulcie left the room she winked in Esther's direction.

By midnight the last soldier had left and Dulcie had gone back down to put the bolt on when there was a knock at the front door. Opening up just a fraction Dulcie was surprised when she saw Doctor Whissey. She had always thought he was a bit weird but still, she couldn't see him wanting to have sex with a young girl.

"Miss Gray I need to speak to you urgently!"

Dulcie opened the door wide and invited the Doctor through into the lounge. The man was uneasy and he fidgeted on the spot. His face was ashen and she could tell that whatever it was he had to say, it would be bad.

"I am so sorry to tell you this but Peggy Spencer passed away this evening."

"Oh my god! She can't have. Fuck me doctor she was only fifty something, if that? It aint no age to go dying."

Dulcie reached out and grabbed the sideboard to steady herself. The tears slowly began to fall and within seconds she was sobbing.

"I know that but after the life she'd led, not that I'm judging, it was no real surprise. Miss Gray she was very ill but didn't realise how ill until it was too late. Now is there anyone else here with you?"

Suddenly an inner strength took over Dulcie and she stood upright. Wiping away her tears she smiled in Bartholomew Whissey's direction.

"I'm fine Doctor really. Now if you will excuse me I have to go and tell the girls."

After showing him out Dulcie slowly made her way upstairs. Esther was the first to be told and although she shed no tears she was aware how much her friend thought of Peggy and so gave her a hug. Bella cried for a moment and Annie merely rubbed at her eyes and then turned over and went back to sleep. Cynthia had been home for only a short while and when informed of the terrible news she just shrugged her shoulders and closed the door on Dulcie Gray.

No clients were allowed into the house for a week as Esther and Dulcie planned the funeral. A couple knocked on the door but much to Cynthia's disgust Dulcie told them to sling their hook. There was almost a row as Cynthia voiced her frustration.

"Well thanks a bunch mate, that's only me Fucking livelihood you're telling to bugger off."

"I tell you what Cynthia; I've held me bleeding tongue for far too long just to keep Peggy happy but not anymore. Show a bit of fucking respect will you. We aint put the poor old girl in the ground yet and you can't wait to get your knickers round your bleeding ankles. What the fucks wrong with you?"

Cynthia Fox couldn't be bothered to argue and besides she could see that Dulcie was in a pig of a mood. The last thing she needed was a shiner and she knew that it was a real possibility if she kept putting the pressure on. Cynthia Fox was as hard as nails, emotionally at least and she had already made her mind up that after tomorrow she would commandeer Peggy's room. It was much larger than her own and if she was going to be the main bread winner, then it was only right she had first dibs on the old girls pad. She knew Bella and Annie would kick up a stink but she was the one who serviced more customers, so in Cynthia's mind that placed her higher up in the pecking order.

The funeral was a dismal affair with only the five young women and Livy in attendance. Dulcie cried for the whole of the service and was consoled on one side by Esther and on the other by her little girl. It was obvious that Bella, Annie and Cynthia didn't really want to be there and at one point Dulcie, from the corner of her eye, spied Bella removing a nail file from her bag.

Did Peggy mean nothing to them? True for all intent and purpose Dulcie supposed the old girl had been their madam but she had also been kind to them, gave them a roof over their heads and this was how they repaid her? She decided to give it a couple of weeks and then things were going to change. Dulcie Gray was going to give her friend her wish and get Esther Goldman her house back and the three were going to live a normal life for once.

CHAPTER TWENTY

It was decided by Dulcie and Esther that they would delay asking Cynthia, Annie and Bella to leave until after Olivia's birthday. Making the girls go would only upset the little one and as it was Livy was sill asking for Peggy. They had both hoped that by keeping her busy she would eventually forget about the woman she had looked upon as a grandmother but they couldn't have been more wrong. Dulcie had explained that Aunty Peggy had gone away but then thought better about telling lies when Livy had started to ask difficult questions. The questions had come like a bolt from the blue and Dulcie hadn't known what to say.
"So where is Aunty Peggy mummy?"
"Well darling she's in heaven."
"Where's heaven mummy."
"Well Livy heaven is a place where we all go eventually. It's a beautiful place and everyone is happy and no one feels any pain."
"Can I go to heaven mummy?"
Dulcie didn't know what to say and looked to Esther for guidance. For the first time her friend couldn't help and only shook her head.
"Baby we will all go there one day but you have your whole life to live. Its only older people who go to heaven darling. Now say a prayer for Aunty Peggy and then it's time for you to go to sleep."

Death wasn't something Livy should have to deal with at her age and Dulcie was at a loss when it came to explaining things properly. Olivia really didn't understand but doing as she was told snuggled down and clasped her hands together. As she spoke, both Dulcie and Esther filled up with emotion at her words.

"Lord keep Aunty Peggy safe in heaven. Please look after mummy and Aunty Esther and make them both strong. Amen. Mummy I don't understand all of this, please ask Aunty Peggy to come to my party."

Livy looked so confused that Dulcie felt like the worst mother in the world. Not knowing how to answer her child Dulcie changed the subject and started to talk about something else.

"Come on Aunty Esther, it's time for a bedtime story don't you think?"

During daylight hours there wasn't anywhere that was out of bounds to Olivia Gray. She could often be found playing in one of the girls rooms or asking to bake cakes in the kitchen with Peggy like she used to. When this question arose Dulcie would change the subject and try to get her daughter interested in something else.

Olivia was approaching her third birthday and a grand party had been planned for Sunday afternoon. It wouldn't be the same without Peggy but three was a special age and one Dulcie didn't want to taint with memories of death and heaven and all that she had been recently trying to teach Olivia about.

It was Saturday night and Cynthia, Annie and Bella had made plans and brought presents, all eagerly anticipating the next day's celebrations. Olivia had been bathed and Esther was putting her to bed. Dulcie liked this time of the day and would watch her child sleep for hours. About to climb the stairs she was stopped when the bell rang. No one else was in the vicinity so she made her way to the door. Outside Cynthia stood on the step accompanied by an American soldier and she was very much the worse for wear.

"Hellooo Dulcie girl Hic!"
"You're pissed Cynthia!"
"So Fucking what?"

Dulcie was too tired to argue and could only manage the wave of her hand in dismissal of the girl. As she climbed the stairs Cynthia and the soldier could be heard in the lounge singing along to Mildred Baileys Scrap your fat. It had been a long day and Dulcie was dog tired. All she hoped for was a warm bed and not too much noise from downstairs. When Dulcie at last reached the bedroom she forgot to bolt the door. It was always the last one in who slid the latch but tonight Dulcie was so very tired. Apart from baking a cake and cleaning the place from top to bottom, she had spent the entire afternoon blowing up balloons and cutting up crepe paper to make decorations for the party. It had been such a long day but she couldn't wait to see her daughters face in the morning. Falling into bed she drifted off to sleep in seconds. It was just past midnight when she woke with a start. For a moment Dulcie rubbed at her eyes and after spying the alarm clock she snuggled close to Esther. About to drift off again, her eyes were suddenly wide open and she searched the bed for Livy. Seeing the open door, terror filled her whole being.

"Esther! Esther wake up, Livy's not here!"

Esther Goldman was a deep sleeper and it took her a moment before it registered what her friend had said.

"Not here? What on earth are you talking about?"

Dulcie was out of the bed in seconds and descended the stairs in record time with Esther following in hot pursuit.

"Livy!! Livy baby where are you?"

The desperation in Dulcie's voice was evident. Esther ran into the lounge and Dulcie into the kitchen. Moments later and a gut wrenching high pitched scream filled the house. It wasn't just the noise that scared Esther but the pain, such a heart breaking pain, the likes of which she'd never heard before.

"Noooooooooooooo!!!!!"

Cynthia Fox was slumped over the kitchen table drunk but it was the sight on the floor that had filled Dulcie Gray with such terror.

The soldier that she had let into the house was now spread eagled on the lino and beneath him Dulcie could make out a small hand, the small perfect hand of her beautiful girl.
"You bastard, you fucking bastard what have you done to her?"
The soldier, who was out of his head on drink, rolled over and began slurring.
"Wos a matter? Wos all the noise about?"
Dulcie fell to the floor and pushing the soldier off, cradled Livy in her arms. Olivia Grays tiny body was lifeless and Dulcie again began to howl. When Esther reached the kitchen she couldn't believe what confronted her. Fear was evident on her face and when she saw the blood on Olivia's legs and nightdress it instantly registered that this beast had interfered with their little girl. A red mist came over Esther Goldman and her mind was filled with rage. Storming over to the kitchen dresser she removed the long handled carving knife that Dulcie always kept extra sharp for Sunday roasts. Dulcie was too deep in her own grief to notice her friend and as Esther leaned over the soldier she plunged the knife into his chest over and over again. Blood sprayed high into the air and he was dead the second the blade made contact with his heart but Esther didn't stop. She continued in an almost frenzied state to stab him again and again. The knife made a sickening squelchy sound with each thrust but both Esther and Dulcie were oblivious to

the noise.

Cynthia Fox had woken up when she heard the awful sound Dulcie was making and as she stood up and saw the carnage she began to scream. "What the fuck have you done to him you leery bitch?"

Esther Goldman had momentarily lost her sanity and as Cynthia approached, she drew the blade sharply across the girls throat. Cynthia Fox clutched at her neck but it was futile. She tried to mouth the word help but no sound emerged. Falling to the floor her legs began to shake and go into spasm. Esther dropped to her knees and started to rock backwards and forwards.

An hour later the two women were still on the floor with Olivia's body. The blood that surrounded them had become sticky and congealed. When the warmth had finally left Livy's tiny frame Esther at last stood up. Trying to pick up Livy she was stopped when Dulcie grabbed her arm. Esther tenderly touched her friends cheek as if to say It's time to move her Dulcie Gray began to weep and wail but she did allow Esther to continue and picking up the lifeless little body she carried her into the lounge. Laying her on the sofa, Esther tenderly wrapped a blanket around their baby girl just as if she was asleep. Inhaling deeply she knew that there was work to be done before she and Dulcie could even begin to grieve properly.

Back in the kitchen Dulcie was still on the floor but

now she just silently stared into space. When Esther spoke to her she didn't answer. Time and again Esther tried to get a reaction from her friend, finally the only thing she could do and it really went against the grain, was to slap Dulcie hard across her cheek.

"Dulcie! We have to clear up before Bella and Annie get back."

"I can't! I can't, don't you understand. Oh Esther my baby girl is dead!!!!!"

"Do you think I don't fucking know that!"

"I'm sorry Esther but I can't do anything, pleeeeeeease just leave me alone. I want my baby oh pleeeeeease god I want my baby!"

Esther Goldman felt helpless. In less than an hour their lives had been shattered, her friend was in so much pain and there was nothing she could do about any of it.

"We have to clear all this blood up Dulcie."

"I can't, I can't."

"Yes you can darling! If we don't get this sorted out well both be on the gallows in Holloway. Please Dulcie, please help me?"

Her friends words at last registered with her and Dulcie Gray got up from the floor. Her hands were thick with blood and she smeared them down her already blood stained dress. Sniffing loudly, she wiped away her tears with the back of her hand and turned to face Esther.

"What do you want me to do?"

"First we need to get rid of these two fuckers. We'll drag them down into the basement till the morning Ok?"
Dulcie nodded and together they hauled the corpses down the stairs. Both women were puffing and out of breath when they'd finally finished.
"Now what?"
"Now we scrub this room from top to bottom and we'd best get a bloody move on as there's no telling what time Bella and Annie will be back."
Dulcie Gray and Esther Goldman cleaned like never before and when they'd finished, the room stank of Jeyes fluid and carbolic soap. They both changed their clothes as quickly as they could, then went into Cynthia's room and collected up all the woman's possessions.
"What shall we do with all Cynthia's stuff?"
"Put it in Peggy's old room for the time being, we need it to look like she packed up and left quickly. Now we must hurry!"
Dulcie had just carried Olivia upstairs and laid her on the bed when the front door opened and the two girls entered.
"Hi there Esther! What a leery night we've had, my fanny feels like its shagged half the bleeding smoke! I bet yours is as bad Annie?"
"You aint wrong there love."
Both girls started to giggle and after everything that had happened, the sound really annoyed Esther.
"Is Cynthia back yet?"

"Been and gone. Packed up all her stuff and just cleared out the ungrateful cow."

"She's gone?"

"Without a by your leave and after all Peggy had done for her."

"So now what do we do, I can't service the whole British army, not to mention the yanks, well not on me own anyway and Annie here, well lately she'd rather spend her time sleeping than shagging."

"The thing is Bella, well me and Dulcie's had a talk and now that Cynthia's gone. Look I'm not going to beat about the bush. We want the house back as a home and not a fucking knocking shop for all and sundry."

"Well! That's gratitude for you."

"You can stay tonight but first...."

"Don't fucking flatter yourself Esther Goldman. If I aint welcome then Ill bleeding go tonight! What say you Annie?"

"Too fucking right! I was starting to get bored with this place anyway. Come on Bella well pack together."

True to their word Bella and Annie had left within the hour and it was a relief in more ways than one for Esther Goldman.

Alone in their room the two women lay down on the bed, one each side of Olivia's tiny corpse. Dulcie didn't know how she'd held herself together and suddenly her pain began to erupt. Dulcie Gray held onto her baby's lifeless little body and broke into

deep racking sobs for what seemed like an eternity. Up early Esther Goldman, her mind now back on track was ready to get things sorted once and for all and had started work in the basement. Dragging first the soldier and then Cynthia, she placed them at the far end of the basement, one on either side of the room. Dulcie came down just in time to see her friend disappear out of the front door. Wandering aimlessly from room to room she was convinced she could hear Livy somewhere. The gnawing pain of last night was still as bad and she felt as though her heart had been torn from her body. Walking through the house and though it made no sense, Dulcie wrapped her arms tightly across her chest and began to talk to Livy.
"I'm sorry baby, mummy should have saved you. I'm so so sorry."
An hour later and Esther finally returned with a young lad in tow.
"Dulcie I'd like to introduce Trevor Smallsworth. Trevor has agreed to bring us a load of bricks from the bombed out houses round the corner. Now then, we agreed a shilling a load so best you get to work."
When the young man had left, Dulcie turned to Esther with a look of confusion on her face.
"I was struggling to lug them back here and he offered to help. I've placed the bodies at the far end of the cellar and I now need to brick them up."
"Brick them up?"

"Look! my darling. No one ever goes in the basement so it's the perfect place to hide them."
"Don't thing you're fucking putting my Livy with them murdering bastards Esther because I aint having it do you hear, I aint bleeding having it."
Esther Goldman was shocked and more than a little hurt to think that her friend thought she could be so insensitive.
"I wouldn't dream of it! After all that we've been through how could you even think such a thing? I loved that child as if she was my own."
Suffering as much as she was, Dulcie still knew she had over stepped the mark and embraced her friend to say sorry. No words were spoken; none were required as they both understood what had been silently agreed.
It took the rest of the day and a lot of toil and sweat by Trevor Smallsworth but at long last Esther had all that she needed.
"I think we have to try and get a few hours sleep, we've got a lot more work to do tomorrow."
Dulcie could only nod and the two friends made their way upstairs. Esther suggested that they sleep in Peggy's old room and that perhaps it was best to let Livy rest in peace. Strangely Dulcie didn't object but the pair slept little that night.
In the morning work again began in earnest. Esther had acquired a bag of lime and instructed Dulcie to liberally cover the bodies with it. Dulcie Grays mind was grieving and although she carried out her

duties, it was in a robotic way and equal amounts of both corpses were left exposed.

Esther Goldman was too busy to notice. After mixing up mortar she diligently laid bricks, a trade taught to her by her father throughout a long hot summer back in her younger years. By nightfall she placed down the last brick and stood back to admire her handy work. A master craftsman she wasn't but Esther Goldman knew that what she'd accomplished was more than adequate and would stand up to the test of time.

Dulcie scrutinized her friends work and even though she was in so much emotional pain, still gave Esther a pat on the back.

The two spent another night in Peggy's room and by the morning they could both smell the onset of decaying flesh.

"Dulcie as much as it pains me to say it, we must lay Livy to rest."

"No please Esther, that's my baby!"

"I know sweetheart but the poor little mite is beginning to smell. If anyone picks up on the scent and there's been enough death in London that it won't be difficult, then were in big trouble. How in god's name would we explain any of this? We can't help our Livy but we can help ourselves, don't you understand that?"

"I know but Oh Esther where can we put her. It's my child, my baby were talking about here!"

"I know love, I know. Yesterday when I was

working down in the basement I noticed some loose flagstones on the floor. It was just as you get to the bottom of the stairs. Far enough away from those bastards that did this and somewhere we can visit and lay flowers. What do you think?"

Dulcie could only nod, she had a lump in her throat and her eyes were brimming with tears.

Early on Tuesday morning the burial of Olivia Gray took place. Both women out of respect wore black and Esther had gone out early and purchased flowers from the market.

The flagstones had been lifted and a small hole dug but even though they'd been well prepared it didn't make the situation any easier. Together they lifted Olivia downstairs but as Esther placed her tiny body into the hole Dulcie began to sob.

"My poor poor baby! This is goodbye, oh Esther I aint ever going to see her beautiful face again."

"I know darling but it has to be done. Come on now say your goodbyes and we can give her the send off she deserves."

Dulcie kneeled on the floor and tenderly place her palm on Livy's chest. Tilting her head up wards she closed her eyes and began to pray.

"Please God, I aint never asked you for nothing in my life before. What I ask now is that you take good care of my angel and keep her close to you. Make her laugh lord, she loves to have her feet tickled in the mornings. Please god tell her that her mummy loves her and one day we'll be together

again. Night night sweetheart. Amen."
The hole was slowly filled in by Esther. After rearranging the flagstones, flowers were placed on top. Dulcie and Esther were now at last ready to leave the basement, though it took all of Dulcie's strength to close the basement door and leave her baby all alone. Olivia Gray was finally at peace but the pain the two women felt was indescribable. Neither Dulcie nor Esther knew if they would be able to carry on.

CHAPTER TWENTY ONE
2001

Finally Dulcie finished talking. Her tea was now stone cold and when she glanced at her watch, realised they'd been in the cafe for over two hours.
"And that Billy boy is my story."
Dulcie raised her head and was expecting to see a look of horror on Billy Jacobs face but all she saw were pools of tears.
"My heart breaks for you Dulcie truly it does."
"There's no need for that love; it was all a long long time ago. They say times a great healer but that aint true. Oh I know as the years pass things aint so raw but you never quite get over it. Just learn to accept it and live your life I suppose."
"So what happened to Esther?"
Dulcie's eyes misted over as she thought back to Esther Goldman.
"Ahh my darling darling friend. Well we stayed at Bell Lane for around fifty years. Neither of us married and a lot of the local kids thought we were a pair of dykes. That always made us smile. No me and Esther were just happy with each other's company. Every Sunday we'd lay flowers on the flagstones at the bottom of the basement stairs. Esther was a good friend to me Billy and when she got Alzheimer's I nursed her right up to the end."
"That's how come you know how to act around Wendy and the others at Green Lawns?"

"Of course it is! Honestly Billy did you think I read it in a medical book or something? and don't keep interrupting me or Ill forget where I was. Anyway with Esther gone I didn't want to stay in the house by myself so I went into care. Just walked into the Royal Free one day and made out I didn't know who I was. That's how come no one knows about the house. I had a piece of paper with me name written on it and that was all."
"So now what do we do?"
"Do? Aint nothing for me to do Billy. I know at the end of this you will do what you feel is right in your heart. The one thing I ask is that if you do decide to go to the Old Bill, let me know first."
"Why?"
"That's none of your business you nosy little fucker but promise me Billy please."
Billy Jacobs could only nod.
"Right then, best we get back before Wendy sends out a bleeding search party."
Billy hailed a cab but they were both deep in thought and the journey was taken in silence. When they reached Green Lawns, Billy turned to Dulcie and gently took her hand in his as they got out of the cab. Escorting Dulcie to her room he tenderly placed a kiss on her cheek.
"I'll see you tomorrow?"
"Maybe you will boy, maybe you will."
Billy Jacobs frowned at his friends choice of words but then shrugged his shoulders and made his way

home. For some reason he had thought that now he knew Dulcie's story and all the pain that she'd been through, well that things would be easier. How wrong he was.

All night long he tossed and turned and when dawn finally appeared he was no further in gaining an answer.

Jackie was in the kitchen frying up some breakfast when her son entered.

"Morning son, sleep well?"

Billy slumped down at the table and placed his head in his hands. Immediately his mother stopped what she was doing and went over to him.

"Whatever's the matter love?"

Billy lifted his head and Jackie could see that he'd been crying.

"Oh come on now sweetheart, things can't be that bad. Have you got a problem at work, don't you like your job anymore son? Have you broken up with Sal?"

"Oh mum whatever am I going to do?"

"Tell me what's happened and maybe I can help. You can, trust me you know!"

Billy could see that she wasn't about to take no for an answer.

"Look someone I know is mixed up in something really bad and I don't know if I should go to the law or not. Trouble is if I don't, then I aint sure I can live with myself."

"Of course you can. Why you and Sally have got so

much to look forward to, that lovely house to move into and......."

"That's just the problem mum."

"What is? Billy you're starting to talk in bleeding riddles now. Look I can't hang about now or I'm going to be late for work. If you aint feeling any better when I get home, well talk some more."

Kissing him on the head Jackie was then about to make her way into the hall but momentarily stopped.

"Billy I never raised you to be a grass but if it's something illegal and someone's been hurt then you have to do the right thing son."

"I know mum."

Jackie hadn't said anything he didn't already know but maybe he just needed to hear that what he was about to do was right."

Unlike his normal swift wash, today Billy Jacobs took his time, anything to avoid doing what he knew he had to do. When he couldn't stand it any longer and all that he'd heard yesterday was fighting to escape his head, Billy left the flat and headed in the direction of the Police station.

At the end of Mentmore Terrace he spied Johnny Drake and Simon Thaxter. The pair were in the process of purchasing something from Remo, the local dealer. Billy couldn't see what it was and he didn't want to. Johnny Drake saw Billy out of the corner of his eye but didn't attempt to make contact. The three hadn't been together for several months

and Billy was happy for it to remain that way. Billy Jacobs had at last grown up. His work at Green Lawns had been a huge factor in his transition from boy to man but the biggest thing had been Dulcie Grays revelation yesterday.
Reaching Sameer's Mini Mart which had been taken over and was now called Price Check, Billy bumped into PC Harry Stanton.
"Well bless my soul if it aint young Billy Jacobs. How are you lad?"
"I'm good thanks."
Harry had been a policeman for over thirty years and when someone was putting on a front he could spot it immediately.
"Well you could have fooled me. Do you want to have a chat; I've just come off shift."
Billy could only nod and the two men walked over to the park in silence. The place, except for a lone dog pawing at the carcass of a pigeon, was deserted. The two men took a seat on one of the graffiti sprayed benches and Harry waited for Billy to speak. Billy Jacobs didn't know how to start and silently concentrated on the ground in front of him.
"So then lad what's troubling you?"
Billy stared deep into Harry's eyes desperately looking for a sign that said you can trust me. There wasn't one.
"Mr Stanton can I ask you a hypothetical question?"
Harry Stanton wanted to laugh. Here was a young lad who'd been on the road to ruin, a lad who just a

few months ago struggled to string a sentence together when talking to the police. Now the boy was a man and to Harry appeared to be a very nice one at that.

"I suppose hypothetical is best. That way you can be honest and not commit yourself, so fire away son."

Billy spent the next half hour telling Harry about the bodies and the sad story of why they were hidden. He didn't mention any names or locations. It felt good to have unburdened himself and he now looked to Harry Stanton for advice.

"Wow! Well lad I can't force you to do anything about this hypothetical problem. What I can say is that those poor souls shouldn't be left to rot in someone's basement. As for the old girl, well in the real world its highly unlikely that the crown prosecutors would do very much, not after taking into consideration her age and the dementia."

Billy nodded his head. He understood what was being said and he knew there really was only one course of action open to him.

"Do you want to make a statement lad?"

"I think I need to Mr Stanton, at least so that I can sleep again."

"Best we get to the station then."

"Will you stay with me?"

"It would be an honour. I'm so proud of you Billy and how you've turned out."

"It's funny Mr Stanton but I don't feel proud, I feel

like the biggest low life on earth. I'm betraying a friend, someone I've come to love."
Harry Stanton tenderly patted Billy on the back. "Sometimes sunshine we have to hurt the ones we love when it comes to doing what's right."
The police interview was over relatively quickly and after Billy, Harry and two C.I.D detectives were taken to Bell Lane, the area soon became a crime scene. Billy was asked to be available for further questioning but apart from that he was free to go. It was obvious to Harry Stanton that the boy was more than a little troubled.
"Can I give you a lift home?"
"Thanks but I need to go and see Dulcie."
"I would strongly advise against it Billy. This is now a murder enquiry and as such you are a potential witness. Going to see Ms Gray could be viewed as corroboration."
"Do you really think I care about that? There's a very old wonderful lady whose about to have her life torn a bleeding part and it's all because of me. The least I can do is fucking say sorry."
Harry Stanton didn't like to hear the young man swear but under the circumstances didn't say anything.
"Best we get you over there then before the detectives arrive."
Billy Jacobs smiled, he liked Harry, realised he was one of the good guys and could be trusted. When they reached Green Lawns the place was in turmoil.

It was Izzy's day off and Wendy had been left in charge. Lawrence was unsuccessfully trying to usher the residents back to their rooms and the scene resembled a lock down at the Scrubs more than a care home. When Wendy spotted Billy the relief on her face was evident.

"Thank the lord! Oh Billy what a bleeding mess and no mistake. When you left Dulcie yesterday was she alright?"

Harry and Billy both looked at each other and Billy raised his eyebrows in a manner that said here we go! Harry smiled and asked Wendy if they could go somewhere private to talk. After the three reached Izzy's office and the door had been firmly closed, Billy Jacobs at last began to speak.

"What's wrong Wendy? Is Dulcie Ok?"

"Fucked if I know. Lawrence went to get her up this morning and her bed hadn't been slept in. Oh Billy she's been missing all night. Izzy's will throw a fit when she gets here. If I manage to keep me job it'll be a fucking miracle."

It was Harry who relayed all that had happened and when he finished Wendy had to hold onto the chair to steady herself.

"Well I never! So for the last five years we've had a murderer on the premises?"

"Please don't call her that Wendy, Dulcie's a good person. She once told me that every action has a reaction. Are you telling me you wouldn't have done the exact same thing if someone had hurt your child?"

Wendy took a moment to think about what was being said and finally she smiled.

"I suppose I would. My Wayne can be a right little wanker at times but if anyone hurt him? Id swing for them."

As much as her words both shocked and warmed Harry Stanton, he knew it wouldn't be long before the detectives arrived.

"Wendy did Dulcie leave anything in her room?"

"Not so much as a bleeding crumb, it's as if she was never here."

"Right do you have a photograph of her?"

Wendy Saxby rummaged through one of the drawers in Izzy's filing cabinet.

"Only this. It was taken a couple of years back at the Christmas party."

Harry studied the snapshot but the faces were fuzzy and Wendy had to point out which one was Dulcie Gray. Added to the fuzziness was the fact that it was a profile image. A hundred pensioners from the street could have been arrested and they would all have resembled her.

"This won't be of any use. Its blurred and the woman could be anyone."

Billy who had been quiet for a while suddenly spoke.

"Is that good Mr Stanton?"

"It is for Dulcie Gray. Now Billy I really think we need to get out of here or were both going to get

charged with interfering with a witness."
As they made their way into the hall Wendy Saxby grabbed hold of Billy's arm.
"Please don't tell me this is the last were going to see of you. Billy you're a good worker, the residents all love you and it would be a crying bloody shame if you left."
Billy Jacobs smiled.
"Wendy nothing could keep me away from this place. I'm going to miss Dulcie, really miss her but it won't stop me coming back to work."
A search was made for Dulcie Gray but after six months and when she hadn't been found, the case went into the back of the filing cabinet along with all the other unsolved cases. True, a nationwide manhunt would probably have located Dulcie and solved the murders but after a police review board had looked into the matter and down to monetary cuts and the fact that it had all happened so long ago, it was deemed not important enough. It would never be closed but all involved knew that it would also never be solved.
Billy kept a close eye on things and any information he needed to know was passed on by Harry Stanton. The bodies had been exhumed but the only one he'd been interested in was that of Olivia Gray. Billy Jackson had used his savings for a cemetery plot and some Sunday afternoons, accompanied by Sally, would lay flowers on the little grave that was marked with a small wooden

cross.

The house on Bell Lane remained empty for several years and was finally demolished, along with the rest of the terrace, in two thousand and ten.

THE END

EPILOGUE

2011
TEN YEARS LATER

Billy was now in charge at Green Lawns Manor. Approaching forty years old he was one of the youngest care home managers in the borough. The Lawns, as he like to refer to the place, was winning award after award for its cleanliness and patient care. Staff and residents alike loved Billy Jacobs and no one would have a bad word said against him. The place was full to capacity; there was even a waiting list for rooms. Occasionally over a coffee Wendy Saxby, who was now his second in command, would bring up Dulcie Grays name but there was never a bad word spoken about the old woman who had lived a life full of tragedy.

It was ten am on a Monday morning and Billy had arrived late to work. Sally had been up all night with their teenage daughter who was suffering stomach cramps. The next day he had decided to take an hour off work to go to the doctors with them.

As he entered The Lawns things as usual were manic but Billy only smiled. Placing his briefcase onto the desk he was about to start sorting out the rotas when he was interrupted by the telephone.

"Green Lawns Manor. Billy Jacobs speaking."

"Oh hello Mr Jacobs its Mary here, Mary Carter.

From social services, you remember we met at last year's Christmas do?"

Billy racked his brains but he still couldn't come up an image of who he was talking to. Never one to be rude he pulled a face that said I aint got a clue who you are.

"Hello Mary how nice to speak to you again."

Likewise Mr Jacobs."

"Please call me Billy, now how can I be of help?"

"Well I know you are always full at Green Lawns and I wouldn't normally ask but..."

"What is it Mary, what's bothering you?"

"We received a telephone call late on Saturday night from the Royal Free. An elderly woman had been admitted in the last stages of dementia. Now I haven't called just because you take dementia patients, though this woman does require twenty four hour care. The consultant said she probably won't last more than a couple of weeks but as there are no beds available in geriatrics I..."

Billy raised his eyebrows, it wasn't that he didn't want to help but simply that he received a phone call like this at least once a day and he just couldn't accommodate everyone.

"I'd like to help Mary but we are absolutely bursting at the moment and..."

"Look Billy I'm not going to beat about the bush! We have no idea who this woman is but in her coat pocket we found a piece of paper with your name on. There was nothing else, no bus pass, pension book, absolutely nothing!"

Billy Jacobs smiled from ear to ear and at the same time a tear trickled down his cheek. He didn't need to hear anymore. Dulcie was coming home and he couldn't wait. Not wanting to seem as if he'd immediately changed his mind, Billy paused for a second.

"I'm sorry Mary I don't have a clue who she is! Hang on a minute; we do have a small room at the back of the house, if that's any good. I can assure you this woman will receive the best care available."

"Oh Billy you're a real life saver. I'll have her brought over by ambulance this afternoon."

Billy opened the office door and called out as loud as he could for Wendy. Seconds later Wendy Saxby came running in and was puffing and panting.

"Whatever's the matter? You nearly gave me a fucking heart attack."

"Dulcie's coming home!"

"Have you been at Edna's sherry again because you aint making any bleeding sense."

Billy Jacobs relayed the entire conversation of a few moments earlier and when he'd finished looked at Wendy with pleading eyes.

"So what you want to know is will I call the Old Bill? of course I bloody wont. That old girls been to hell and back, what good would calling
the police do?"

Billy grabbed Wendy by the arms and began to dance around the room laughing.

It didn't matter that Dulcie probably wouldn't recognise him; all he cared about was seeing his old friend again.

That day at two pm precisely, an ambulance turned into the driveway of Green Lawns Manor. Billy and Wendy were outside apprehensively waiting to greet their newest resident.

Billy was a little nervous when the doors were at last opened. He was worried at what state Dulcie would be in; worried that maybe he wouldn't even recognise her but his fears turned out to be unfounded. Even though she was asleep, she still looked exactly as she had eleven years earlier.

When the ambulance crew had placed her into bed and Billy and Dulcie were alone in the small room, Billy bent down and placed a tender kiss on the old woman's face.

"Stop fucking slavering over me you cheeky little fucker."

Dulcie Gray had once again conned all those around her and Billy Jacobs began to laugh.

"Why you crafty old cow!"

"Nothing crafty about it Billy Boy, it's called survival."

Wendy Saxby had been attending to Ruby out in the hall when she heard the laughter and shaking her head she just smiled. Dulcie Gray didn't have dementia but she was very frail. At every opportunity Billy Jacobs would pop in and visit but the topic of her past was never mentioned. Billy didn't want anyone or anything to upset Dulcie in her final days. On a Sunday afternoon, the day before she died, Billy wheeled Dulcie over to

the cemetery. When she saw the tiny grave that Billy and Sally had so lovingly cared for all these years, Dulcie smiled and squeezed her friends hand. No words were spoken, none were needed.
The following morning Billy opened Dulcie's bedroom door to say hello but it was too late. Sometime in the night Dulcie Gray had peacefully slipped away. It broke Billy's heart to lose her again but he sought consolation in the fact, that finally Dulcie had found peace and was once more reunited with Olivia and Esther.

February 14th 2012 (2am)

"And that Olivia, is my little story."
"Did you really know this Dulcie woman dad?"
"I did indeed and I'll tell you something else Livy, they broke the mould when they made her."
"Why didn't I meet her?"
"She was old Livy and very frail. Now I told you that story for a reason, so did you understand what I was trying to get at?"
"I think so. Like what you said at the beginning, every action has a reaction."
"Exactly, now try and get some sleep or your mums going to be on the warpath in the morning and I for one don't want to be on the receiving end."
"Thanks dad you've really helped me, maybe I won't say them things about Lucy after all."
"Good! Now go to sleep."
"Love you dad."

Billy Jacobs laughed to himself.
"I love you too Livy, sweet dreams darling."

Printed in Poland
by Amazon Fulfillment
Poland Sp. z o.o., Wrocław